GH STBUSTERS

Kicked out of Columbia University because of their shoddy research methods, Doctors Peter Venkman, Raymond Stantz and Egon Spengler go into business under the name of Ghostbusters just as an epidemic of ghouls descends on New York City. With homemade machines to zap and trap ectoplasmic visitors from the netherworld, the Three Stooges of parapsychology are off to their geigercounters in extra-terrestrial disturbances.

Reviews from America

'*Ghostbusters* is irresistible . . . inspired lunacy'

'A cute, rip-roaring good time comedy'

'The maniacal trio pass into a state of pure silliness bordering on the divine, which never once wavers'

'A lunatic parody of supernatural horror, sci-fantasy and poltergeists'

'Supernatural fun. It has madly silly dialogue and some deft, witty and wily performances'

'*Ghostbusters* is outlandish, delicious fun'

'A complete delight'

'Side-splittingly funny'

GHOSTBUSTERS

Novelisation by

LARRY MILNE

**Based on the Screenplay by
Dan Aykroyd and Harold Ramis**

**CORONET BOOKS
Hodder and Stoughton**

Copyright © 1984 by Columbia Pictures Inc.
Stills by courtesy of Columbia Pictures
Lyric copyright © 1984 by Ray Parker Jr.

First published in Great Britain 1984
by Coronet

British Library C.I.P.

Milne, Larry
Ghostbusters.
I. Title
823'.914[F]   PR6063.06/

ISBN 0-340-37251-6

Printed and bound in Great Britain for
Hodder and Stoughton Paperbacks, a
division of Hodder and Stoughton Ltd.,
Mill Road, Dunton Green, Sevenoaks,
Kent (Editorial Office: 47 Bedford
Square, London, WC1 3DP) by
Richard Clay (The Chaucer Press) Ltd.,
Bungay, Suffolk. Photoset by
Rowland Phototypesetting Ltd.,
Bury St Edmunds, Suffolk.

COLUMBIA PICTURES

Presents

AN IVAN REITMAN FILM

A BLACK RHINO/BERNIE BRILLSTEIN PRODUCTION

BILL MURRAY
DAN AYKROYD
SIGOURNEY WEAVER

'*GHOSTBUSTERS*'

HAROLD RAMIS
RICK MORANIS

Music by ELMER BERNSTEIN. Production Design by JOHN DE CUIR. Director of Photography LASZLO KOVACS, A.S.C. Visual Effects by RICHARD EDLUND, A.S.C. Executive Producer BERNIE BRILLSTEIN. Written by DAN AYKROYD and HAROLD RAMIS. Directed and Produced by IVAN REITMAN.

GHOSTBUSTERS

1

A beautiful Manhattan morning. Breathe deep and you can smell the carbon monoxide fumes tumbling along Fifth Avenue. On the corner of Fifth and 42nd Street, the photo-chemical smog nibbles at the classical façade of the New York Public Library.

The twin stone lions, guardians of knowledge, bask serenely in the lethal sunshine. Moth-eaten pigeons flutter and scramble for scraps amongst the students and native New Yorkers lounging on the broad steps.

An ordinary day. Nothing to get excited about.

Sad to say that nothing remotely exciting has happened to creaky old Miss Ellis, spinster-librarian of this parish, in over six decades, not counting that incident on VJ Night, 1945.

There she goes now, slightly stooped, straight greying hair framing a careworn face, wheeling her cart of books through the sepulchral calm of the reading-room. Green-shaded lamps form pools of deep study and golden silence.

Clutching an armful of books to her shapeless bosom, Miss Ellis heads for the basement. The iron spiral staircase leads her down into the labyrinth of stacks. There are miles of them, but Miss Ellis knows her way blindfold. Humming a little tune, she plods along the narrow musty aisles, unaware that this ordinary, unexciting day is about to change . . .

Something is down there in the stacks with her.

Behind her back a book detaches itself from a shelf. Sails silently across the aisle. Inserts itself unobtrusively in the shelf opposite her. Another does the same. Several of the other books get the same idea and silently swap places.

Happily oblivious, Miss Ellis plods on past a wooden cabinet of card index files. As she does so, one of the drawers slides open and a shower of cards flips into the air.

Though partially deaf, Miss Ellis hears the sound and stops dead. She turns. She frowns. Her eyes narrow with suspicion.

Some nasty person is playing tricks. Messing up her sacred files and littering her private domain. Probably, she thinks, that new young trainee, Lyle what's-his-name.

Miss Ellis squares her jaw and squints into the dimness.

Then, right in front of her eyes, another drawer opens, as if pulled by an unseen hand. Cards pop up and shoot out everywhere. In a trice the epidemic spreads and more drawers slide open. More cards cascade into the air. The aisle becomes filled with a whirling snowstorm of index cards.

Miss Ellis whimpers, drops her books, and backs away, deeper into the stacks. Weighty tomes are flying everywhere. Cards are showering down all around her. The basement of the New York Public

Library is going crazy. Her horoscope said nothing about this.

Truly frightened now, Lyle or no Lyle, Miss Ellis turns and staggers on spindly legs between the enclosing walls of books. For a minute she panics, losing herself in the musty labyrinth. And as she turns a corner almost wets her pants.

Her wrinkled mouth goes slack.

Her eyes go round and glassy with terror.

Her gnarled hands clutch each other in supplication.

An intense white light bathes her in a ghostly aura.

But who can she call?

2

'Now I'm going to turn over the next card and I want you to concentrate and tell me what you think it is.'

Dr Peter Venkman raises a quizzical eyebrow at the First Year student sitting across the table from him. An associate professor in the Department of Parapsychology at Columbia University, Venkman can best be described as sleazy charm in a rumpled suit. His mocking smile and laid-back manner more than compensate for a yawning gulf in scientific discipline and academic achievement.

Not that Venkman gives a damn about either at this precise moment. For sitting next to the goofy First Year kid is a ravishing blonde Co-ed with green eyes and the sexiest lower lip on campus.

'Ready?' Venkman asks, taking an ESP card from the top of the pack. At the student's wary nod, Venkman holds the card up in his left hand, face side showing a star symbol towards himself.

'All right. What is it?'

The student frowns, concentrating hard. 'A square?'

Venkman shakes his head sadly and shows the card.

'Good guess – but no.' He presses a button on the end of a cord and the student jumps as an electric shock passes through the wires taped to his fingertips.

Venkman gives his attention to the girl and looks deeply into her green eyes. 'Now just clear your mind and tell me what you see,' he says gently, holding up a card with a circle, again hidden from the view of his two student volunteers.

'Is it – a star?'

Venkman rocks back in fake surprise. 'It is a star! That's great. You're very good.'

He slides the card back into the pack and faces the student. 'Now think,' he says, holding up a card with a diamond on it.

The student clears his throat and glances nervously at the electrodes on his fingertips. 'Circle?'

'Close.' Venkman shakes his head sympathetically. 'But definitely wrong.' And presses the button. The student jumps several inches off the chair and scowls at Venkman. He'd wondered why someone had written 'Venkman Burn In Hell!' on the door of the Paranormal Studies Laboratory, and now it's becoming clear. The man is an out-and-out sadist.

Venkman smiles at the girl and selects another card for her – a triangle this time. 'What about this one?'

The girl bites the sexiest lower lip on campus. 'Ummm –' she plunges '– figure eight?'

Venkman is staggered. He slips the card back into the pack before anyone can see it and says in awed tones, 'Incredible! Five for five.' He eyes her shrewdly. 'You're not cheating on me here, are you?'

'No, really,' says the girl, opening her green eyes wide. She shrugs. 'They're just coming to me.'

'Well, you're doing great,' says Venkman admiringly. 'Keep it up.'

Now it is the student's turn again. He grits his teeth as Venkman selects another card and holds it up Two parallel wavy lines.

'Nervous?'

'Yes,' the student says sullenly. 'I don't like this.'

'Well, just seventy-five more to go,' Venkman tells him cheerfully. 'What's this one?'

The student takes a deep breath and screws his eyes tightly shut, concentrating for all he's worth. Then:

'Two wavy lines?' he says hopefully.

Venkman loses the card at once, shaking his head briskly.

'Sorry. This isn't your day.' He stabs down on the button and the student yelps and leaps up. He's had it. Enough is enough.

He says angrily, 'Hey! I'm getting a little tired of this!'

'You volunteered, didn't you?' Venkman says, with hurt surprise. 'Aren't we paying you for this?'

'Yeah, but I didn't know you were going to give me electric shocks.' The student stands glowering at him. 'What are you trying to prove?'

Venkman puts on his serious academic expression, or as near as he can manage it with features habitually accustomed to covering up lies and stratagems and deceits.

'I'm studying the effect of negative reinforcement on ESP ability.'

'I'll tell you the effect!' the student rages. 'It's

14

pissing me off!' He rips the electrodes from his fingers and stalks angrily across the lab to the door.

Venkman nods. 'Then my theory was correct.'

'Keep the five bucks. I've had it,' says the student, and departs.

Venkman sighs and runs a hand through his thinning hair. 'Well,' he says philosophically, 'I guess some people have it and some don't.'

The girl with green eyes pouts her gorgeous mouth at him.

'Do you think I have it, Dr Venkman?'

The associate professor of parapsychology thinks this girl has everything. And would like some of it for himself.

He moves swiftly round the table and sits next to her, taking her hands in his. 'Definitely,' he says with soulful intensity. 'I think you may be a very gifted telepath. But what you have to realise – it's the kind of ability that could bring resentment. You'll have to be very careful –'

What the green-eyed blonde Co-ed will have to be very careful about remains stillborn as the door crashes open to admit Ray Stantz, Venkman's close colleague and best friend.

A beefy, energetic man with a thick mane of dark hair, Stantz is obviously in a hurry. He lopes across the lab, wrenches open a cupboard, and starts rummaging inside.

Without looking up, he says urgently, 'Drop everything, Venkman. We got one.'

Venkman pats the girl's hand. His smile is strained. 'Excuse me for a minute,' he says, getting up.

He goes across to the corner cupboard and smacks

his close colleague and best friend smartly across the head, though Stantz is too preoccupied to notice.

'Ray, can't you see I'm right in the middle of something here?' Venkman says in a low, sexually-deprived voice. 'Can you come back in about an hour?'

Stantz hauls a mass of electronic equipment out of the cupboard and straightens up. The eternal optimist to Venkman's seedy opportunism, Stantz is buzzing with suppressed excitement.

He dumps the equipment on top of the cupboard and leans forward, the light of the genuine man of science burning in his eyes.

'Peter – at 11.40 this morning at the main branch of the New York Public Library on Fifth Avenue, ten people witnessed a free-roaming, vaporous, full-torso apparition. It blew books from the shelves at twenty feet away. Scared the socks off some poor librarian.'

Venkman gives a brief knowing smile.

'Sure. That's great, Ray. I think you should get down there right away and check it out. Let me know what happens.'

He turns away and Stantz grabs his arm.

'No, this one's for real, Peter. Spengler went down there and took some PKE readings.' Stantz's grip is hurting Venkman's arm. 'Right off the top of the scale! Buried the needle. We're close this time. I can feel it.'

Venkman rubs his jaw and considers

He looks at Stantz and then at the girl, the perfect study of a man torn between duty and pleasure. He'll take pleasure any day, but Stantz has started to convince him that this just might be important. He decides.

'Okay. Just give me a second here.'

Venkman comes up with the appropriate look of pained regret, which isn't difficult, and crosses back to the girl.

'I have to leave now, but if you've got some time I'd like you to come back this evening and do some more work with me. Say about . . .'

The lovely blonde girl beams at him brightly. 'Eight o'clock?'

Venkman stares at her in disbelief. 'I was just going to say eight.' He shakes his head, filled with admiration. 'You're fantastic!'

Later he seriously intends to find out if this is true.

3

Venkman is first out of the taxi and already striding up the steps of the Public Library while Stantz, loaded down with equipment, is struggling to get through the door of the cab. Typically thorough, he's brought everything: infra-red camera, psychokinetic energy (PKE) sensor, ectoplasmic detector, and a whole battery of sophisticated aural and visual sensing devices.

If there's anything remotely supernatural in the New York Public Library, Stantz is going to find it.

He catches up with Venkman, puffing slightly but still alight with the thrill of the chase. 'Spengler and I have charted every psychic occurrence in the Tri-State area for the past two years. The graph we came up with definitely points to something big.'

'Ray,' Venkman says frankly, 'as your friend I have to tell you I think you've really gone round the bend on this ghost stuff. You've been running your ass off for two years checking out every schizo in the Five Boroughs who thinks he's had an experience.' Venkman's crumpled face wears a pained expression. 'And what have you seen? What?'

'What do you mean by "seen"?' says Stantz cautiously, following him through the main door.

'Looked at with your eyes.'

Stantz is on the defensive. 'Well, I witnessed an unexplained sponge-like creature in Queens once . . .'

'Uh-huh. I've heard about the "sponge-like creature", Ray.' Venkman casts a meaningful glance at his friend. 'I think you've been spending too much time with Spengler.'

The Spengler in question is on his knees in the main reading-room listening to a table. Tall and lanky and intense, with thin metal-frame spectacles perched on a bony nose, Dr Egon Spengler has more brains than he knows what to do with. He combines the qualities of incredible intelligence and breathtaking naïvety – which helps to explain how and why he single-handedly got Venkman through graduate school. Ever generous, Venkman's heartfelt gratitude is expressed by feeding Spengler the occasional chocolate bar.

Spengler moves the stethoscope pad along the wooden table-top, listening raptly through stereo headphones for psychic vibrations. And there they are! A steady rhythmic beat from the spirit world. He's made contact!

The contact happens to be with the flesh-and-blood Venkman, rapping with his knuckles on the table to attract Spengler's attention. When this doesn't work, Venkman slams a heavy dictionary down which nearly shatters Spengler's eardrums.

The tall scientist leaps to his feet, wrenching off the headphones. 'Oh – you're here,' says Spengler in his deep mournful voice.

Venkman nods patiently. 'What have you got, Egon?'

'Oh, this is big, Peter. This is *very* big. There's definitely something here.'

Venkman has heard this before. Many times. He sighs and walks on, with Spengler and Stantz following in his wake.

'Egon, somehow this reminds me of the time you tried to drill a hole in your head. Do you remember that?'

'It would have worked if you'd let me finish,' Spengler tells him with an air of regret.

The head librarian, an agitated young man with a heat rash in a three-piece suit, appears. Nervously, he casts sidelong glances at the raised faces of the readers under the green-shaded lamps, who are obviously curious about this disturbance to their peaceful routine.

'Hello, I'm Roger Delacorte, the head librarian,' he says, keeping his voice low. 'Are you the men from the University?'

'Yes,' says Venkman, shaking hands. 'I'm Dr Venkman and this is Dr Stantz.'

The head librarian swallows with relief and hurries them along to his office. 'Thank you for coming. I'd appreciate it if we could take care of this quickly and quietly.'

Venkman pauses in the doorway. 'One thing at a time. We don't even know what it is yet.'

Already he's taken a vague dislike to Mr Delacorte.

These civil-servant types were all the same – they didn't mind trouble as long as it was dumped on someone else. Anyone else.

Prim little Miss Ellis, who had the 'experience', is lying back on a couch, being treated for shock. She is white to the gills. Sending Spengler off to continue the search, Venkman and Stantz settle down to listen to her story.

Whatever it was she saw – or thought she saw – without doubt would have turned her hair grey, if it wasn't grey already.

Venkman, however, is his usual sceptical self. Spirits and spooks in the New York Public Library! Ridiculous! He sits and listens with barely-concealed impatience.

'. . . I don't remember seeing any legs – but it definitely had arms because it reached for me . . .'

'Arms! Great!' Stantz bounces up and down jubilantly, a big fat grin on his face. 'I can't wait to get a look at this thing!'

Venkman gives him a sour sidelong glance and hunches forward, speaking to the woman directly.

'All right, Miss Ellis. Have you or has any member of your family ever been diagnosed schizophrenic or mentally incompetent?'

Miss Ellis is doing her level best to be helpful. 'Well, my uncle thought he was St Jerome.'

Venkman looks knowingly at Stantz. 'I'd call that a big "yes".' Then back to Miss Ellis. 'Do you yourself habitually use drugs, stimulants or alcohol?'

'No.'

'Somehow I didn't think so. And one last thing. Are you currently menstruating?'

Mr Delacorte's eyes protrude out of his head. 'What's that got to do with it?' he wants to know, shocked to the core.

'Back off, man!' snaps Venkman laconically. 'I'm a scientist!'

A patter of feet outside and Spengler sticks his head in, his eyes wide and excited behind his wire-frame spectacles.

'It's moving!'

Venkman and Stantz exchange startled glances and dive for the door. This they have to see.

4

Silence. Darkness. Musty decay.

On tiptoe, Venkman, Stantz and Spengler, in reverse order, descend the iron spiral staircase into the basement. The stacks stretch away into the impenetrable distance. You can hear their hearts beating and Venkman's hair getting thinner.

Spengler unhooks his PKE sensor and holds it up – a slim black device with two spoke-like antennae which extend and light up when there's any psychokinetic energy in the immediate vicinity. So far there isn't.

So far so good, Venkman thinks, fingers crossed.

Around the next corner Spengler stops and beckons the others forward. They stand and gawp. In the exact centre of the aisle is a single stack of books reaching to the ceiling. Stantz is impressed. 'Would you look at this?' he says in a voice hushed with awe.

'No human being would stack books like this,' Venkman agrees, deadpan. With a shake of the head, he sighs and moves on.

All three stop and listen as a faint creaking sound intrudes into the heavy silence. And suddenly, without warning, a full stack of books topples over right on top of them. They leap out of the way through a choking cloud of dust.

If there is a spook, Venkman doesn't like its sense of humour.

But now Spengler has spotted something. The open empty drawers of the card index files, sticking out like rude tongues. And covering them a horrible slimy substance which is dripping in long glutinous strands to the floor.

'Ectoplasmic residue,' Spengler notes, leaning forward to sniff at it. 'Take a sample, Peter.'

With patent disgust, Venkman scoops up a gob of the stuff and scrapes it into a small greaseproof container. 'Somebody blows their nose and you want to keep it,' he complains, handing the container to Spengler. 'Egon – your mucus.'

But Spengler has other things on his mind. The lights on the sensor have started winking and the antennae are slowly extending as they detect an ethereal presence.

'It's here,' he murmurs, pointing to a dark aisle a few feet away.

Creeping forward, hardly daring to breathe, the three of them peer round the corner. And sure enough, there it is.

A middle-aged woman in an ornate wig, and wearing a period gown, is quite calmly reading a book. Nothing too remarkable about that, except that she's floating three feet off the ground and they can see right through her.

If the others can't believe their eyes, Venkman is totally stunned. As an associate professor of parapsychology, he's always had a healthy disbelief in the supernatural.

Mesmerised, he nudges Stantz. 'What is it?' he says in a rusty whisper.

'A full-torso, free-floating apparition.' Stantz swings his camera up and starts taking infra-red pictures. He's like a kid on Christmas morning. 'I told you it was real!'

'Yeah. But what do we do now?'

'I don't know.' Stantz shrugs his quarterback's shoulders. 'Talk to it.'

Venkman drags his eyes away from the apparition. 'What do I say?'

'Anything! Just make contact.'

Venkman edges forward. He licks his dry lips and takes a deep breath.

'Hey, lady?' He cowers back a little as the apparition turns, but seems to look right through them. He tries again. 'Lady? Where are you from – originally?'

The figure turns and raises a finger to her lips. 'Sshhhh!' she says softly.

'This isn't going to work,' Venkman says, stepping back. 'Think of something else.'

Stantz gathers them together. 'Okay, okay. I got it. I know what to do. Stay close. I have a plan.'

With the others on either side, watching him for a sign, he begins slowly to creep forward. Halting a few feet away from the spectral figure, Stantz whispers, 'Okay, do exactly as I say. Everybody ready?'

The other two nod. They're glad Stantz has a plan. Good old Ray. 'Ready.'

'Okay,' says Stantz. 'GET HER!!'

Stantz leaps, arms outstretched, and in a spasm of

pure automatic reflex, so do Venkman and Spengler. All three sail clean through the floating phantasm and land in a heap on the floor. Unfortunately, having disturbed the lady's reading, they've also made her mad.

Because suddenly, the middle-aged lady in the gown is gone – and in her place appears a huge red skull spewing a hot fiery blast. The dreadful spectre blows them along the aisle, like a raging demon pursuing the souls of the damned.

Scrambling on all fours, our heroes beat a hasty retreat back to the spiral staircase. They don't stop there. They don't stop at Mr Delacorte's office. They don't stop in the reading-room.

They don't stop until they're outside – and then only to hail a cab.

Venkman is disgusted. '"Get her". That was your whole plan?' he remonstrates with Stantz, as the three of them walk back across campus to the Paranormal Studies Lab. 'You call that science?'

'I guess I got a little overexcited,' Stantz admits. His long potato face breaks into an ecstatic grin. 'Wasn't it incredible! Peter, I'm telling you, this is the first. You know what this could mean to the University?'

'Oh yeah,' says Venkman with a fine edge of sarcasm. 'This could probably be bigger than the microchip.' He sweeps his hand out at the surrounding buildings. 'They'll probably throw out the entire engineering department and turn their facility over to us. We're probably the first serious scientists ever to molest a dead old lady.'

Spengler offers another point of view. He's been busy working out the sensory data on the mini-computer he wears round his neck.

'I wouldn't say the experience was completely wasted. Based on these new readings, I think we have an excellent chance of actually catching a ghost and holding it indefinitely.'

This hits Venkman like a bombshell and stops him in his tracks while Spengler and Stantz continue merrily on their way. Trap a ghost? Has the man gone out of his gigantic brain?

'Then we were right!' Stantz enthuses. 'This is great – and if the ionisation rate is constant for all ectoplasmic entities, I think we could really kick ass. In the spiritual sense.'

Venkman catches up as they go down the steps and enter the Parapsychology Department. He finds himself a little breathless. 'Spengler, are you serious about actually catching a ghost?'

'I'm always serious,' says Spengler seriously, peering at him down his long nose.

'Wow.' Venkman's mind is reeling with fantastic possibilities, like for instance winning the Nobel Prize. Of course, being by nature a generous person, he'd see to it that Spengler and Stantz were given credit for their supporting roles.

'Egon, I take back everything I ever said about you. Take this. You've earned it.'

Spengler's eyes light up and he grabs the offered chocolate bar and is stuffing it into his mouth as they enter the lab.

The place is a shambles. Workmen are dismantling the equipment and wheeling it out. Venkman is pushed aside by a burly maintenance man carrying a CRT display. He sizes up the situation at once and strides over to Dean Yaeger, who is checking off the inventory on a clipboard.

These two are adversaries from way back. Fighting down his anger, Venkman says curtly, 'I trust you're moving us to a better space on campus?'

With more teeth than his mouth can comfortably accommodate, Dean Yaeger's smile is like that of a basking shark.

'No, Dr Venkman, we're moving you *off* campus. The Board of Regents has decided to terminate your grant. You are to vacate these premises immediately.'

'This is preposterous! I demand an explanation.'

'Fine. This University will no longer continue any funding of any kind for your group's activities.'

'But why? The students love us!'

Dean Yaeger lays down the clipboard and folds his arms.

'Dr Venkman,' he says quietly, 'we believe that the purpose of science is to serve mankind. You, however, seem to regard science as some kind of "dodge" or "hustle". Your theories are the worst kind of popular tripe, your methods are sloppy, and your conclusions are highly questionable. You're a poor scientist, Dr Venkman, and you have no place in this department or in this University.'

Venkman isn't usually lost for words, but right at this moment all he can find to say is, 'I see,' which sounds pretty feeble coming from the man they call 'the Mouth'.

5

His round pudgy face propped in the palm of his hand, Ray Stantz slumps disconsolately against the stone balustrade fronting Weaver Hall, which houses the University's Department of Psychology. At ten o'clock this morning the future looked rosy; now it's in ruins.

'This is like a major disgrace . . . forget MIT or Stanford now,' he moans, gazing emptily towards the skyscrapers of lower Manhattan. 'They wouldn't touch us with a three-metre cattle prod.'

For a man who's just lost his job, Venkman seems remarkably unconcerned. He takes a swig from a half-pint bottle of Scotch and grimaces with pleasure as the glow infiltrates his insides. He offers the bottle to Stantz, who shakes his head moodily.

'You're always so worried about your reputation,' Venkman chides him. 'We don't need the University. Einstein did his best stuff while he was working as a patent clerk.' He waves the bottle nonchalantly, dismissing all the academic might of Columbia University. 'They can't stop progress.'

'Do you know what a patent clerk makes?' Stantz stares at him from under shaggy beetling brows. 'I

29

liked the University. They gave us money, they gave us the facilities, and we didn't have to produce *anything*!' He slumps back morosely. 'I've worked in the private sector. They expect results. You've never been *out* of college. You don't know what it's like out there.'

Venkman takes another slug of whisky and taps him on the shoulder.

'Let me tell you, Ray, everything in life happens for a reason. Call it fate, call it luck, karma, whatever.' There is a strange visionary spark in his eyes. 'I think we were destined to get kicked out of there.'

'For what purpose?'

Venkman wears a narrow crafty grin. 'To go into business for ourselves.'

Stantz blinks. The idea is attractive, but at the same time strewn with snags. He says doubtfully, 'I don't know, Peter. That costs money. And the laser-containment system we have in mind will require a load of bread to capitalise. Where would we get the money?'

But Venkman has thought of that too.

He claps Stantz on the shoulder as the three of them emerge from the granite portals of the Chase Manhattan Bank and step out into the Avenue of the Americas.

Venkman is jubilant. Stantz is worried. Spengler is working out figures on his mini-computer.

'You'll never regret this, Ray!'

'My parents left me that house. I was born there.'

'You're not going to lose the house,' Venkman soothes him. 'Everybody has three mortgages these days.'

'But at nineteen per cent interest!' Stantz is distraught. 'You didn't even bargain with the guy.'

Spengler presses a button and checks the read-out in the illuminated display.

'Just for your information, Ray, the interest payments alone for the first five years come to $94,000.'

Stantz groans.

'Will you guys *relax*?' Venkman says, throwing up his hands. He thumps his palm with his fist. 'We are on the threshold of establishing the indispensable defence science of the next decade. Paranormal Investigations and Eliminations.' He strides confidently along, dodging dawdling pedestrians. 'The franchise rights alone will make us wealthy beyond your wildest dreams.'

'But most people are afraid to even report these things,' Stantz points out.

'Maybe.' Venkman grins. He's given some thought to that as well. 'But no one ever advertised before.'

Before they can advertise, however, there's the problem of finding premises in the heart of New York City. Two days later, after calling half-a-dozen real estate agents, Venkman comes up with what he thinks is the perfect location: a square, four-storey abandoned fire station built around the turn of the century.

The plump young lady in the Century 21 blazer shows them round. The frontage, on a dingy street, is none too appealing, with its faded red paint and a legend in chipped gilt letters which reads: 'Engine Company No. 93'. Inside the wide double doors a white-tiled garage bay extends back to a repair shop. Still in place is the shiny brass pole, disappearing through a hole in the ceiling to the firemen's quarters on the floor above.

Venkman crinkles his nose at the foisty smell of disuse. He wants the place, it feels right, but he doesn't want the woman in the blazer to know it. He listens with feigned indifference as she rhymes off the old firehall's appointments.

'Besides this, you've got another substantial work area on the next floor, office space, sleeping quarters and showers on the floor above that. And you have your full kitchen on the top level. It's 10,000 square feet in total.'

Spengler comes through from the partitioned office at the back, fingers busy with his computer.

'Actually, it's 9,643.55 square feet,' he corrects her, pushing his glasses more firmly on to his nose.

The plump young lady moves her gum to the other side of her mouth. 'What is he – your accountant?' she asks with a frown.

'This *might* do,' Venkman says hesitantly, as if racked by doubt. 'I don't know. It just seems kind of pricey, don't you think? We're trying to keep our costs down,' he explains, favouring her with his most charming smile. 'You know how it is when you're starting a new company.'

'Sure, I know. What are you calling your business?'

Venkman glances at Spengler. Then turns to the young lady.

'Ghostbusters.'

If he's expecting a reaction, he doesn't get it. She swaps her gum and says blandly, 'Oh, well, this place is perfect for it.'

Venkman signals with his eyebrows to Spengler.

At this rate they're going to have to pay top dollar.
Spengler comes to the rescue.

'Miss, have you taken into account this building's
grave defects?' he says in his funereal voice, and
begins to list them. 'Beam structure faulty, wiring
substandard, floors subsiding, dry rot in the woodwork, plumbing disconnected . . .'

Venkman nods happily. This is more like it.

'Whheeee!!' yells Stantz, making his appearance
through the hole in the ceiling and sliding down the
brass pole to land at Venkman's feet, a big childlike
grin pasted from ear to ear.

'This place is great! Just what we need. When do
we move in? And this pole still works!' he says,
wrapping himself round it.

Venkman rolls his eyes and reaches for his cheque-
book, drawing blood from his lower lip.

33

6

Like a minnow escaping from a shoal of barracuda, the taxi peels away from the bumper-to-bumper traffic on Central Park West and turns into the relatively quiet backwater of 78th Street. With a squeal of brakes it stops outside a high-rise apartment building which at first sight appears to be a remnant stage-set from a Busby Berkley musical.

Rising some forty storeys, the Gothic structure is topped by the marble columns and polished dome of what appears to be a temple of some kind, complete with an altar and a flight of stone steps leading up to a pair of bronze doors, inlaid with dull gleaming copper.

Strangely and more ominously, a pair of huge mythical horned beasts worked in stone stand on pedestals, guarding the portal. With left paws raised, talons extended, they stare with blank stone eyes across the towers and canyons of Manhattan.

Seen in the slanting light of the late afternoon sun, the temple structure and the petrified beasts possess a quality of disturbing unreality, and also of menace. As if, lost in another time, they are simply awaiting the day, the hour, the moment, when at last they will be called upon to fulfil their rightful, dreadful destiny.

Still, it has a great view of Central Park.

Which is one of the reasons why Dana Barrett, the stunningly attractive girl stepping out of the cab, chose to live there in the two-bedroom apartment on the thirty-fifth floor.

Dana juggles a bag of groceries and an awkward cello case while she tries to pay the driver. She's had a hard day rehearsing with the New York Philharmonic over at Lincoln Center. That Second Movement of Mahler's Fifth was a bitch.

Now, she thinks, rising smoothly in the elevator, she'll take a hot scented bath, relax in her satin robe, and put some mellow Stan Getz on the stereo. She's had quite enough of brooding Austrian angst for one day, thank you.

This plan meets its first setback as Dana walks tiredly along the corridor, the heavy cello dragging at her arm.

The setback comes in the unprepossessing shape of Louis Tully, her neighbour three doors along the hallway. Ever since she moved in, Louis has been carrying a torch for Dana that dwarfs the Statue of Liberty's. Most evenings he waits behind the door, all five-feet-nothing of him palpitating and perspiring, for Dana's return.

Dana has tried – and still tries – to be kind to Louis, recognising the symptoms of a hopeless and unrequited passion, although tonight she has to summon up all her patience to deal compassionately with the Nerd of the Thirty-fifth Floor.

'Oh, Dana, it's you,' says Louis, peeking out, as if caught by surprise. 'I thought it was the drugstore.'

Despite her better judgment, Dana halts. 'Are you sick, Louis?'

'Oh, no, I feel great,' Louis says, hustling forward, and in his eagerness not hearing the door slam behind him. 'I just ordered some more vitamins.'

His thin, pale, peaky face is upturned to hers in anxious adoration. Dana Barrett is the most gorgeously sexy creature Louis has ever encountered. Tall and slender, with long legs right up to her firm posterior, she has all the style and cool grace of Louis's idealised modern woman: talented, independent, and with a determined tilt to her jaw that tells the world and Louis that Dana Barrett knows what she wants.

Louis wishes it was him; every night he dreams of being raped by her. He gulps and says, 'I was just exercising. I taped "20-Minute Work-out" and played it back at high speed so it only took ten minutes and I got a really good work-out . . . you wanna have a mineral water with me?'

'No thanks, Louis. I'm really tired. I've been rehearsing all afternoon.' Dana smiles and moves on.

'Okay. I'll take a raincheck.' Louis runs along beside her. 'I always have plenty of mineral water and other nutritious health foods – but you know that. Listen, that reminds me, I'm having a party for all my clients. It's gonna be my fourth anniversary as an accountant. I know you fill out your own tax returns but I'd like you to come, being that you're my neighbour and all . . .'

'Oh, that's nice, Louis,' Dana murmurs, fumbling for her key. 'I'll stop by if I'm around.'

'You know,' Louis continues unabated, making the most of the opportunity, 'you shouldn't leave your TV on so loud when you go out. That creep down the hall phoned the manager.'

'I thought I turned it off.' Dana frowns and listens. She can plainly hear the sound through the door. 'I guess I forgot,' she shrugs, inserting the key in the lock.

'I climbed on the window-ledge to see if I could disconnect the cable but I couldn't reach, so I turned up the sound on my TV real loud so they'd think there was something wrong with everybody's TV . . .'

Dana slips into her apartment with a brief wave.

'. . . you know, you and I should really have keys to each other's apartment,' Louis burbles, as the door closes gently but firmly in his face. 'In case of emergencies . . .'

He wanders back to his own apartment to discover the door is locked.

'. . . like this one.'

Dana dumps her cello next to the couch. She's halfway to the kitchen with the groceries when she remembers the TV and goes to switch it off. Her fingers pause on the knob.

A man with a dumpy potato-like face steps up to the camera, holding a weird-looking probe device. He's dressed in some sort of combat uniform.

'Are you troubled by strange noises in the night?' Stantz says in a cheerful booming voice. 'Do you experience feelings of dread in your basement or attic? Have you or your family actually seen a spook, spectre, or ghost? If the answer is yes, then don't wait another minute.' He points a commanding finger. 'Just pick up the phone and call the professionals – Ghostbusters.'

The scene changes to Venkman, Stantz and Spengler outside the old fire station. A neon sign above their heads shows the children's cartoon figure of Caspar the Friendly Ghost inside a red circle with a diagonal red bar across it – the international symbol of prohibition. All three are wearing jumpsuits, covered in zips and pouches.

Spengler steps forward and salutes.

'Our courteous and efficient staff are on call twenty-four hours a day to serve all your supernatural elimination needs.'

Then the camera zooms into a close-up of the three of them wearing fixed cheesy smiles, and they chant in unison:

'We're ready to believe you!'

As a telephone number is supered on the screen, Dana leans over and flicks it off. *Supernatural elimination needs?* Can they be serious? In New York, of all places?

In the kitchen she unpacks the groceries and places a carton of eggs and a loaf of bread on the plastic counter-top. After the experience with Louis, that long hot bath seems more inviting than ever. But first get rid of these, she decides, reaching up to open the corner cupboard.

Stifling a yawn, she puts away a jar of coffee and a packet of brown sugar. Behind her back the lid on the carton of eggs flips open. The two neat rows of eggs start to vibrate. Then shake. An egg leaps out and smashes on the counter-top. A second does the same, and a third. And as they shatter they start to sizzle.

Dana glances over her shoulder and gives a startled gasp. Eggs are frying on her counter-top . . . perfectly ordinary eggs on her perfectly normal counter-top. And yet – as if that weren't odd enough – when she touches it with tentative fingers, the plastic is quite cool, almost cold in fact.

Standing in the middle of the kitchen, Dana stares at the frying eggs with dark mesmerised eyes. There has to be a rational explanation. The only trouble is, she can't for the life of her think of one.

Her heart leaps in her chest as something nearby gives a low, deep-throated growl. It is her refrigerator.

Her refrigerator is growling at her.

Edging towards it, Dana reaches out at full stretch and grasps the chrome handle. It feels reassuringly solid in her hand. Part of her tells her not to do it. Another part tells her not to be so stupid. People aren't frightened of their fridges. This is the twentieth century. The age of reason.

The firm jaw that Louis so admires stiffens with resolve. The hell with it. She yanks the big white door wide open.

Dana staggers back as a blood-red blast of heat and light pours into the kitchen. The inside of the fridge is a fiery inferno. Shafts of light pierce a swirling crimson mist and dazzle her eyes with fantastic shapes. The growling is very loud now, as if issuing from the jaws of a demon hound of hell.

Somewhere in there she can see a flight of stone

steps, and beyond, shimmering through the heat, a pair of bronze temple doors.

The doors begin to open. From deep within comes a hoarse whisper that makes the blood congeal in her veins. Not of this world, it fills her head with a single word –

'ZUUL!!'

Dana screams and slams the door shut.

7

Venkman stands back and proudly surveys the freshly-painted sign above the garage doors. 'GHOST-BUSTERS', it reads, in red letters two feet high on a yellow ground.

The place is shaping up nicely. Maintenance bay cleaned and swept, office refurbished, all major repair work completed, and a spanking new paint job on the front of the building. The sign is the perfect finishing touch. Now they're really in business.

That's if there *is* any business, Venkman reminds himself glumly. The TV commercials had eaten a big hole in their capital, and still not a single enquiry.

He turns with a frown of annoyance as an antiquated Cadillac ambulance rumbles up and parks right outside the door. The bumpers are hanging off and the dull black bodywork is scratched and dented. On the roof, the emergency lights are cracked and twisted on their brackets.

Venkman raises his hand and bangs on the bonnet. 'You can't park here, fella!'

'Everybody relax,' says Stantz, sticking his potato head out of the window with a big goofy grin. 'I found the car. How do you like it?' he asks, jumping out and closing the door carefully on its single hinge.

Venkman gazes with dismay at the huge decrepit monstrosity.

Blue smoke rings rise from the rear end. This thing alone is making a major contribution to environmental pollution. 'How much?'

'Forty-eight hundred.'

That should just about clear the kitty, thinks Venkman, putting his weight on the nearside front wing. The Cadillac wallows drunkenly and groans like something in pain.

Even this doesn't dampen Stantz's enthusiasm.

'Just needs a little suspension work,' he says cheerfully. 'And a muffler . . . and maybe brakes. And new shocks . . . transmission . . . engine mountings. And possibly a rear axle . . .'

Upstairs, in the first floor office, Janine Melnitz presides over the silent switchboard. For the third time that morning she paints another coat of red polish on her nails. Pert and petite, with short dark hair, she peers near-sightedly at her handiwork through a pair of large spectacles perched on the tip of her cute snub nose.

Venkman mooches by on his way to the open-plan office behind the reception area. The sight of Janine with nothing to do annoys him. 'Any calls?' he mumbles.

Intent on her thumbnail, Janine shakes her head slowly, not bothering to look up.

'Type something, would you?' Venkman says irritably. 'I'm paying for this.'

Janine pulls a face behind his back. Spengler's head

pops up from under the desk. He has a screwdriver in his teeth and holds a bunch of multicoloured wires.

'You're very handy, I can tell,' Janine says brightly. 'I bet you like to read a lot too.'

'Print is dead,' says Spengler shortly.

'That's very fascinating to me,' Janine says in her broad Brooklyn accent. 'I read a lot myself. Some people think I'm too intellectual. But I think reading is a fabulous way to spend your spare time.' She inspects the finished nail critically. 'I also play racketball. Do you ever play?'

Spengler crawls out, having finished the wiring job. He gazes down at her vacantly, his lower lip jutting out, a sure sign that his tremendous brain is struggling to grapple with the real world. Nobody has ever bothered to explain the facts of life to Spengler; he worked them out for himself on a pocket calculator and vaguely suspects he came up with the wrong answer.

'Is that a game?'

'It's a *great* game! You should play some time. I bet you'd be good.' Janine appraises him. 'You seem very athletic – do you have any hobbies?'

'I collect spores, moulds and fungus.'

'Oh.' Janine's smile slips a little. 'That's very – unusual.'

'I think it's the food of the future.'

'Remind me not to go to lunch with you,' Janine says, returning to her nails.

Ten minutes later she's into some serious reading when a tall, lithe young woman with a soft cloud of curly auburn hair enters through the swing doors and approaches the desk rather hesitantly. Janine hurriedly lays the *National Enquirer* aside and sits up straight, the model of bright-eyed and bushy-tailed efficiency.

'Is this Ghostbusters?' Dana Barrett asks, glancing round doubtfully at the plain green walls and flaking plaster ceiling. Already she's beginning to regret this.

Before Janine can frame a reply, Venkman has leapt up from behind a row of filing cabinets and cleared the rail bordering the office area in a single leap. Not only their first customer, but *what* a customer! She has to be the most beautiful girl he's ever seen in his entire existence. Venkman is instantly, hopelessly, in love.

He skids to a halt, smoothes back his hair, straightens his tie, and says in a tone of suave intimacy:

'Hello – I'm Peter Venkman. May I help you?'

'Yes, well . . . I'm not sure.' Dana hesitates. 'What I have to say may sound a little –' she shrugs her slender shoulders and Venkman endures ravening pangs of lust '– unusual.'

'We're all professionals here, Miss . . .'

'Barrett. Dana Barrett.'

Venkman takes her hand in his sweating palm and leads her through. 'Why don't you step into the office and we'll talk about it.' He opens the gate. 'Hold all my calls, Janine.'

'What calls?' Janine replies, returning to the black pit of boredom and the *National Enquirer.*

'So what do you think it was?' Venkman asks, leaning forward intently, elbows on his knees. He watches her closely as Dana attempts to give the question serious consideration.

Under the circumstances – not to mention Venkman's rabid scrutiny – Dana is finding this somewhat difficult.

Lie-detector pads are taped to her temples. A video camera is recording her every facial expression. And she is surrounded by three young men, one of whom – this brashly confident Venkman character with the quizzical eyebrows – seems to have other things on his mind than getting to the bottom of her problem.

If she's seen it once, she's seen that glint a thousand times.

Bringing her mind back to the question, Dana answers thoughtfully, 'I think something in my refrigerator is trying to get me.'

Venkman exchanges glances with Stantz and Spengler. Then focuses back on Dana. 'Generally, you don't see that kind of behaviour in a major appliance.'

Dana's flawless forehead puckers in a frown. The corner of her mouth twitches in a smile. She can't make this guy out. Is he a genuine scientist or a charlatan with a quicksilver tongue?

'She's telling the truth,' Spengler chips in, studying the polygraph read-out. 'Or at least thinks she is.'

'Why would anyone make up a thing like that?' Dana asks, offended.

'Some people like the attention,' Venkman tells her. 'Some people are just crazy.'

Stantz gets up and starts pacing. 'You know, Peter, this could be a past life experience intruding on the present.'

'Or even a race memory, stored in the collective unconscious,' Spengler adds. 'And I wouldn't rule out clairvoyance or telepathic contact either.'

Dana looks from one to the other and then bursts out laughing. She sobers quickly as the three faces regard her sternly.

'I'm sorry – it's just that I don't believe in any of these things. I don't even know my sign.'

'You're a Scorpio with your moon in Leo and Aquarius rising,' says Spengler, referring to his notes.

'Is that good?'

Venkman leans closer, and cocks an eyebrow. 'It means you're bright, ambitious, outgoing and very, very sexy.'

Dana narrows her eyes shrewdly. She got his number right first time. Venkman interprets the look as a provocative 'maybe' and gulps almost audibly.

'Were any other words spoken that you remember?' he asks huskily, looking into her eyes.

'No, just that one word – "Zuul". But I have no idea what it means.'

Spengler is frowning over his notes. 'I'll see if I can find any reference to that in the literature. Tobin's *Spirit Guide. Theory of the Science of Spirits.*'

'Good idea,' says Venkman mechanically.

'Why don't I check out the building?' Stantz suggests. 'It may have a history of psychic turbulence.'

'Great,' says Venkman, rising and helping Dana remove the pads. 'And while you're doing that I'll take Miss Barrett home and check her out.' He clears his throat and smiles glassily. 'I mean, check out Miss Barrett's apartment.'

Dana slips into her coat and turns to go. Venkman moans under his breath. He does a nervous little dance of sexual longing and rolls his eyes towards heaven.

What a job.
What a woman.
What an opportunity.

8

As Dana unlocks the door of her apartment, Venkman raises a cautioning hand. He taps his chest and points, indicating that he will go first. Dana nods: go ahead.

What is he expecting? The Phantom of the Opera?

He sidles through the door and creeps forward, Dana close behind. The window gives a panoramic view of the park. The trees cast long spiky shadows from the setting sun. The living-room is in semidarkness and rather eerie, though otherwise appears quite normal.

Gaining in confidence, Venkman ventures further into the room and bumps into a piano. He lifts the lid and tinkles a trill of high notes, explaining, 'They don't like this; drives them wild.'

Dana leans nonchalantly against the wall and lifts a sceptical eyebrow. She's still waiting for the 'expert' to swing into action.

Venkman does. Whipping out his ecto-wand, he pumps the rubber bulb at one end, extending the rod into a long probe, which he wafts about in an aimless fashion. An invention of Spengler's, the ecto-wand is supposed to detect any psychic presence. Unfortunately, Venkman hasn't a clue how it works. No matter. It looks pretty impressive, he feels.

'Have you ever thought of moving out – at least until this disturbance blows over?' he asks Dana.

'No.' Dana's shake of the head is firm, definite. 'If I moved out now I'd be acknowledging that what happened was real. I'm not ready to do that.'

Venkman nods and wafts the wand some more. Dana leans her head on one side and says, 'What is that?'

'This?'

'That.'

'It's – uh – technical.'

'Are you sure you're using it properly?'

Venkman gives a feeble grin and points to a door. 'What's in there?'

'That's the bedroom,' Dana says, taking off her coat and hanging it up. 'But nothing ever happened in there.'

Venkman casts an appreciative eye over her neat figure in blouse and pleated skirt. 'That's a crime,' he mutters.

'What?'

'Nothing.' He wanders round the room, poking the wand here and there.

Dana stands with her arms folded, not in the least impressed by this performance. She taps her heel a few times and says, 'Hadn't you better check out the kitchen? It's that door there.'

Venkman seems extremely reluctant. He's not sure what he's looking for, and what's more, he doesn't wish to find it. But now he's here, he has little choice.

He pushes open the kitchen door and Dana follows

49

him in. The cooked eggs are stuck to the counter-top, hard and crinkly, like staring yellow eyes.

'This is quite a mess.'

'I told you, I –'

'I know. It happened by itself,' Venkman says, scanning the room with his wand. 'Nothing.'

'That,' Dana says, pointing it out, 'is the refrigerator,' as if the six-feet-tall appliance might have escaped his attention. 'Are you going to look inside?'

Venkman's bluff has been called. He squares his shoulders and grips the handle of the fridge manfully. Putting his face close up to it, he opens the door the tiniest crack and squints inside with one eye. Then rears back, his face contorted with horror.

'Ugh!'

'What is it!' Dana exclaims, clenching her fists, her heart in her mouth.

'Junk food,' Venkman says with disgust, holding up a roll of shrink-wrapped processed liverwurst between finger and thumb. 'Do you really eat this stuff?'

Dana has had enough – of Venkman and his wand.

'Look, are you going to investigate this – this thing or not? Because if not –'

She takes one look at Venkman's mildly bemused face and turns on her heel and storms out of the kitchen. Venkman goes after her. Always a firm believer in the direct approach, he catches up with her at the couch and doesn't hesitate.

'I'd better come right out and say it. I'm madly in love with you.'

Dana whirls round. The angry gleam in her eyes has laughter dancing round the edges of it. She's never met anyone quite like Venkman before. She opens her mouth and closes it again. Finally, all she can think of to say is, 'You are so odd.'

Venkman just shrugs and gives her his crumpled smile.

'You really don't act like a scientist.'

'No? What do I act like?'

'Like a game-show host.'

'Thanks,' says Venkman sourly. He flops down in a chair. 'I'm a qualified psychologist and parapsychologist. I've got degrees and everything. I believe that something happened here and I want to do something about it.'

'All right.' Dana nods slowly, prepared to give it another shot and Venkman the benefit of the doubt. 'What do you want to do?'

'I think I should spend the night here.'

'That's it. Get out.'

'On a purely scientific basis.'

Dana raises her finger like the barrel of a gun and points to the door. 'Out!'

Venkman appeals to her. 'I want to help you.'

'I'll scream.'

Venkman gets up quickly. 'Don't scream.'

'Then leave,' Dana says, marching to the door and wrenching it open. There she waits, one hand on her hip, the colour high in her cheeks.

'Okay, okay.' Venkman holds up his hands. In the doorway he turns and says, with a belated attempt at seriousness, 'But if anything else happens, you have to promise you'll call me.'

'All right.'

'Then I guess I'll go,' Venkman says, as the door closes in his face.

'Goodbye,' says Dana firmly. Venkman's head appears round the edge of the door, eyebrows raised hopefully.

'No kiss?'

Dana slams the door and shoots the bolt home.

Janine switches off the desk lamp and picks up her handbag. Her fingers sag wearily with the weight of nail polish she's applied. And if she reads another story about Joan Collins, she'll scream.

So much for the exciting prospect of working for an outfit of professional ghost-catchers. She's had more excitement watching the freezer defrost.

She reaches for her coat in the darkened office, and as she shrugs into it, the phone rings.

'Yeah, Ghostbusters,' says Janine boredly. 'Yes, it is. Yes, of course they're serious . . .'

Her mouth drops open and her eyes light up. 'You do! You have! Yes, *sir*.' She hunts for a pencil and starts scribbling furiously. 'Yeah, I have it . . . right . . . don't worry, they'll be totally discreet, sir.'

Janine hits an alarm button and jumps up and down, waving the paper aloft.

'We got one! We got one!'

9

The alarm bell shrills through the building. In the living quarters, Stantz and Spengler leap to their feet, scattering cartons of chow mein and garlic shrimps in all directions. They collide in the doorway, disentangle themselves and stagger through into the locker room.

Venkman charges in from the dorm. No time to talk, or even to think. All three grab their jumpsuits and climb into them. They leap for the brass pole and – one – two – three – hit the garage bay in a flurry of arms and legs.

Strapping on heavy proton drive backpacks, they clip particle throwers to their belts and grab ecto-containment traps from the power chargers. Fully kitted-up, infra-visors in position, straps tightened, harnesses double-checked, and they're ready to go!

The garage doors slide back and the broken-down black Cadillac roars into the dark street. Only it's no longer a broken-down black Cadillac. Not any more. No sir.

Now it's been transformed into a gleaming silver Ectomobile!

A flashing purple-and-white strobe display lights

up the dingy back alleys. Communication antennae spin on the roof. On the doors, the Friendly Ghost symbol is emblazoned in red and white.

As the Ectomobile heads uptown, giving off a weird ultra-violet aura, the low unearthly moan of its siren echoes throughout the city. Inside, three jubilant and nervously excited ectoplasmic exterminators.

Their first-ever real assignment.

Stand by, New York City.

The Ghostbusters are on their way!

The manager of the Hotel Sedgewick, striped bow tie and thin freckled hands, meets them in the lobby. He steers them through quickly, groaning inside at the fuss and speculation their appearance is causing amongst his fashionable clientele.

He wasn't expecting this. Not dressed in those ridiculous combat-style uniforms. And with their tinted visors and all that heavy equipment strapped to their backs, looking like a cross between a welder and something out of *Star Wars*.

Still, he's desperate. He gathers them round, speaking in low and agitated tones. 'The guests are starting to ask questions and I'm running out of excuses. Can you do something quickly?'

'Has this ever happened before?' Stantz enquires for the record.

'Well, most of the original staff knows about the twelfth floor . . .' The manager sneaks a scared glance over his shoulder. 'The disturbances, I mean. But it's been quiet for years . . . up until two weeks ago. It was never ever this bad, though.'

'Did you ever report it to anyone?' asks Stantz, jotting down notes.

'Heavens no!' The manager shudders at the thought. 'The owners don't like us to even talk about it. I hoped we could take care of this quietly tonight.'

Stantz is brisk and businesslike.

'Yes, sir. Don't worry,' he says reassuringly. 'We handle this kind of thing all the time.'

The manager smiles wanly and watches as the three of them stump across the lobby to the elevator. Venkman stabs the button with his gloved finger, demonstrating a confidence he doesn't feel. What the hell is he getting into here?

'What are you supposed to be?' asks a portly gentleman in a dinner jacket, smoking a large cigar, waiting for the elevator.

'Me?' says Venkman, turning. 'We're the – uh – the exterminators. Somebody saw a cockroach on the twelfth floor.'

The man appraises their heavy proton packs and lethal-looking particle throwers with bulging, slightly bloodshot eyes.

'That's gotta be some cockroach.'

'Well, you can't be too careful with those babies,' Venkman tells him as the elevator doors open. 'Coming up?'

The man shakes his head hurriedly. 'You go ahead. I'll get the next one.'

Crowded into the elevator, their bulky equipment taking up most of the room, all three start to sweat. Up until this moment this ghost-hunting caper has been a bit of a gag. None of them has taken it totally seriously. Now it's for real.

Stantz clears his throat as if he's swallowed a ton of sawdust. 'I just realised something. We've never had a completely successful test with any of the equipment.'

'I blame myself,' Spengler says, his long face set in a frown.

'So do I,' says Venkman.

'No sense in worrying about it now, I guess,' Stantz says, looking on the bright side.

'Sure,' Venkman shrugs. 'Each of us is wearing an unlicensed nuclear accelerator on our back. No problem.'

'Try it,' Stantz urges. 'Start me up.'

Spengler does so and the elevator begins to rattle and shake from side to side as the proton pack builds up from a low pulsating whine to a shrill pounding crescendo. Any second now and they could have a compact nuclear explosion on their hands.

Venkman passes a trembling hand over his eyes. Spengler wears his doubtful frown. Stantz just looks sick.

10

The twelfth-floor corridor is deserted. This makes Venkman feel slightly easier. With all the high-powered atomic weaponry they're carrying, innocent bystanders could easily get hurt.

He nods to the others and all three draw their snub-nosed particle throwers and flip down their ecto-visors. Spengler is taking valence readings with his PKE meter. So far there is no activity – the twin antennae are retracted, the lights dead.

In line abreast, they advance along the corridor. It is deathly quiet. But not for long.

A squealing and rattling sound comes from directly behind them, and in a single sweeping movement Stantz whirls round and sends a glistening, looping coil of quantum energy searing along the corridor. Venkman, his nerves screwed up to snapping point, reacts on reflex and sprays his beam wildly in the same general direction. Ion particles fizz and crackle. The air is acrid with discharged neutron energy.

The three of them peer anxiously through the smoke and charred strips of wallpaper floating down, leaving wispy trails.

On her knees and hugging the carpet, an elderly

cleaning woman sticks her prune-like face round the edge of a trolley and stares at them with wrinkled, incredulous eyes. The contents of the trolley have been totally wasted. Broken bottles glug cleaning fluid on to the carpet. A large pack of toilet rolls is on fire.

Shamefaced, Stantz lowers his weapon. 'Sorry, madam.'

'We'd better adjust our streams,' Spengler cautions.

They're getting nowhere fast. 'Better if we split up,' Stantz says, glancing at the others.

'Yeah,' says Venkman, looking round at the charred wallpaper, the blackened ceiling, the smouldering carpet. 'We can do more damage that way.'

They decide to each take a separate floor. Stantz stays on the twelfth. The Sedgewick is bigger than he realised. Five minutes later he's checked two of the main corridors and still nothing.

He fishes out a pack of cigarettes and is in the act of lighting one when the needle on his PKE meter swings clear across into the red. Stantz goggles at it, and breathes into the button mike of the transceiver strapped to his chest:

'Egon! Peter! I got something! I'm moving in!'

PKE meter held in front of him, particle thrower at the ready, Stantz advances with slow, careful tread to the next corner. He flattens himself to the wall. Pokes his head round. And stands rooted to the spot, gaping through his ecto-visor at the Ghost of the Twelfth Floor.

The thing is like a vaporous yellow sack with a

panic, and gibbers into the mike, 'Well, I think you guessed wrong. Here it comes!'

Stantz leaps down the stairs, five at a time. Over the headset comes a terrifying shriek that curdles the marrow in his bones. He dashes through a doorway, turns a corner, and spies Venkman on his back in the middle of the corridor, arms and legs flailing the air like a helpless insect.

A glutinous, sickly yellowish-green substance is spread like a thick goo over his head and chest.

'Aaaarrggghhh – aaarrggghhh –' Venkman quivers convulsively and sucks in a shuddering breath. 'It slimed me! It slimed me!'

Stantz drags him to his feet. Over the headset come Spengler's mournful tones, heightened an octave to a pitch of dreadful excitement.

'Ray – it's here! It just went into the Banquet Room on the third floor!'

Stantz rushes back to the stairway and Venkman trudges after him, leaving a trail of ectoplasmic slime.

11

Spengler is waiting for them outside the Banquet Room. And so is the manager, wringing his freckled hands and hopping from foot to foot. He has a function due to start in fifteen minutes for two hundred people. Can this be dealt with quickly, quietly and unobtrusively? he pleads.

Stantz brushes him aside and pushes the door open with his combat boot. Venkman and Spengler take up positions on either side of the door. When he sees they're ready, Stantz raps out:

'Visors down. Safetys off. Full stream.'

Tucking in his chin pugnaciously, Stantz darts swiftly into the large darkened room, the other two fanning out behind him.

Round tables covered with crisp white linen, set with gleaming silverware and sparkling goblets, loom like islands in the dimness. A faint purple sheen reflects off the satin-draped walls. High above, in the centre of the ornately-moulded ceiling, a huge and magnificent crystal chandelier gathers the room's dim light and gives it back in tiny shimmering glints.

Stantz drops to one knee.

'There! On the ceiling!'

He raises his thrower as Venkman and Spengler scuttle forward. All three take aim. A fat yellowish haze with a malevolent grin flits behind a curved beam.

'Come on down here, you slug!' Stantz yells, and releases a curling etheric strand of glistening particles. The vapour dodges nimbly away and half the chandelier disintegrates. Venkman fires blindly, destroying the other half. Fragments of pulverised crystal tinkle over the tables.

'Wait! Wait!' Spengler stops them with a frantic wave of his hand. 'There's something I forgot to tell you.'

'What?'

'*Don't-cross-the-streams.*'

'Why not?'

'Trust me,' Spengler says. 'It will be bad.'

Venkman exchanges glances with Stantz. 'What do you mean, "bad"?'

Spengler's high forehead knits in a studious frown. 'It's hard to explain, but try to imagine all life as you know it stopping instantaneously and every molecule in your body exploding at the speed of light.'

Venkman blinks slowly and looks away.

'Glad you mentioned it, Egon. Good safety precaution.'

They switch their attention back to the vapour, hovering near the ceiling, and Stantz says grimly, 'This thing's not going to hang around all day waiting for us. Pete, give me one stream wide to the right of it. I'll go wide left. Okay?' Venkman nods. 'Now!'

They trigger off two streams either side of the vapour, trapping it between the ceiling and the wall.

Bolts of energy blast great blackened holes and scorch the silken wall-drapes into tattered smouldering strips. The tables are now wrecked and strewn with chunks of plaster and flaming debris.

Stantz talks them through the wholesale demolition of the Banquet Room.

'Good . . . good . . . nice and wide . . . move with it . . . easy . . . hold steady . . .'

The vapour bobs and weaves between the streams, Venkman and Stantz delicately adjusting their aim to keep it boxed in.

'Now, very slowly, Pete . . . let's tighten it up. You hold steady . . . I'm coming in . . .'

The quantum streams drift dangerously close.

'Don't cross them! Watch it!' Spengler warns.

The streams get closer still, and almost touch.

'I'm losing it! I'm losing it!' Venkman panics.

'Spengler – a little help!' Stantz shouts. 'Cut it off!'

But Spengler's marksmanship is even poorer. He sends a stream within centimetres of Venkman's, who has to jerk away abruptly, searing a sizeable portion of oak panelling in the far corner.

Pacing the corridor outside, the waxen-faced manager winces at the sound of crashing plaster and smashing glass and other extensive property damage. He wonders numbly about early retirement.

Luckily, Stantz has finally mastered the technique, and is holding the bulbous yellow phantasm in a swirling cocoon of energy particles.

'You got it!' Venkman encourages him. 'That's good, Ray. Easy now.'

'All right,' says Spengler calmly, 'I'm going to throw the trap now. Ready?'

Keeping his eyes on the vapour, he reaches behind him and unhooks the ecto-containment trap from his belt. This is a small rectangular device, about eighteen inches long, painted with diagonal yellow-and-black warning stripes. Fed by a cable from the proton pack, it has a row of PKE indicator lights set into the titanium steel, lead-lined casing.

Very slowly and carefully, Spengler lays the trap down on a clear area of floor. Stantz edges backwards, manoeuvring the vapour into position.

Venkman holds his breath. 'Easy . . . easy does it . . .'

'Okay.' Stantz sneaks a glance over his shoulder. 'Open the trap – now!'

Spengler thumbs a button. There is a loud, high-pitched electronic buzz. A beaded curtain of intense white light, in the shape of an inverted pyramid, springs up from the device, enclosing the yellow haze, which writhes and squirms like a tormented spirit inside the force field.

Suddenly there is a blinding flash of pink light. The beaded curtain of light has gone, and so has the yellow vapour. Leaving just a puff of brackish brown smoke and some wisps of carbonised particles floating to the ceiling.

For a long moment there is absolute silence.

The Ghostbusters stand in a limp semicircle, staring uncertainly at the trap. Then Spengler gingerly leans forward and peers at the valence indicators. He turns and looks at the other two.

'It's in there.'

Venkman and Stantz flip up their steamy visors and whoop in triumph. They did it! *They did it!*

Stantz says with a broad beaming grin, 'Well – that wasn't so bad, was it?'

For an answer, Venkman gives him a baleful glare and wipes the ecto-slime from his sleeve.

The Ghostbusters emerge from the Banquet Room to find two hundred guests in evening clothes milling about. A low murmur of curiosity and polite alarm ripples through the crowd at the strange appearance of these three weary, stained and dishevelled front-line troops.

'What happened?' asks the manager, pushing his way through and mopping his brow. 'Did you see it? What was it?'

Stantz proudly holds up the ecto-containment trap. The manager steps back a pace and wafts the air as he catches a whiff of the putrid yellow fumes drifting from the innards.

'We got it!' Stantz grins at him triumphantly.

'But what was it? Will there be any more of them?'

'Sir, what you had there,' Stantz tells him, 'was what we refer to as a focused non-terminal repeating phantasm. Or a Class Five Full-Roaming Vapour. A real nasty one, too.'

'That'll be four big ones for the entrapment,' Venkman says, writing out the bill, 'and this month we have a special offer on for proton recharge and storage – only $1000.'

'Five thousand dollars!' the manager says, aghast, staring at them with bulging eyes. 'I won't pay it. I had no idea it would be so much!'

Venkman nods. 'Fine. We'll let it go again.' He turns to Stantz. 'Ray, put it back.'

'No! No!' the manager squeaks. 'All right. Any-thing.'

Venkman hands him the bill with a sweet smile. 'Happy to be of service, sir. Feel free to call us again if you need us.'

The Ghostbusters are in business.

12

Not only in business, but big news.

It seems as if not only New York City, but the entire nation, has suddenly discovered spooks and spirits. Woken up to ghosts and ghouls. Gone wild on poltergeists and precognition. Etheric doubles and ESP. Clairvoyance and corporeal vision and things that go bump in the night.

From coast to coast, in every newspaper and magazine, on every TV network and radio station, the story catches fire as the country goes on an unprecedented paranormal spree . . .

Hello, America! This is Ronald Gwynne reporting from United Press International in New York. Throughout my entire career as a journalist I have never reported anything as exciting and incredible as the trapping of an actual supernatural entity by a team of men based in this city who call themselves Ghostbusters. Now, most of us have never even heard of a floating, slime-like substance called ectoplasm, but these gentlemen claim we will be seeing a lot more of it than ever before.

Splashed across the covers of *Time* and *Newsweek*, the Ghostbusters become the most famous trio of faces in the United States. Personality pieces, photo spreads and in-depth analyses proliferate in everything from *People* to the *Washington Post*.

And along with the media attention, a strange phenomenon, as phantasms and psychic presences start popping up out of the woodwork . . .

Good morning, this is Roger Grimsby, with the NBC News. Today the entire Eastern Seaboard is alive with talk of hundreds of reported incidents involving multiple sightings of what can only be described as extreme events of paranormal extra-phenomenical proportions. It seems everybody is willing to bring their old ghosts and skeletons out of the closet. Roy Brady reports from New York.

The scene switches to the old fire station, where the media have set up camp. Behind Roy Brady, newsmen, television crews and radio reporters besiege a harassed-looking Venkman, Stantz and Spengler beneath the neon sign of everyone's favourite Friendly Ghost.

Thank you, Roger. Everybody's heard ghost stories around the campfire. Heck, my grandma used to spin yarns about a spectral locomotive that used to rocket past the farm where she grew up. Now, as if some unseen authority had suddenly given permission, thousands of people are talking about encounters they claim to have had with ghosts.

Dressed in their ecto-suits, the Ghostbusters field questions from a scrambling mêlée of reporters, while police barriers hold back a surging, excited crowd.

'Nate Cohen. I'm with the *Post*. Did you really trap a ghost?'

'We sure did,' Stantz affirms.

'Can we see it?'

'Uh . . . I'm afraid not.'

'Is this some kind of stunt?' asks another newsman.

'This is not a sideshow,' answers Venkman sternly, wearing his affronted academic face. 'We're serious scientists.'

'What proof do you have that what you saw was real?'

'Proof?' exclaims Stantz. 'Well, the manager of the Sedgewick paid us five big ones to get *something* out of there. Is that real enough for you?'

A radio reporter thrusts a mike under their noses. 'Tell us about those guns you're wearing.'

'They're not guns,' Spengler corrects her. 'They're particle throwers.'

'Can we see one working?'

Spengler shakes his head. 'We couldn't do that, Miss. Someone might get hurt.'

'Sing the song from your commercial,' a TV reporter calls out, pointing them to a mini-camera. When they appear reluctant, he wheedles, 'Come on. It's free advertising . . .'

The appeal touches Venkman's soft spot, and he mutters in an aside, 'There's a thought. Hit it, Ray.'

Stantz turns a mottled pink, and with great effort starts singing down at his boots:

'There's something strange in the neighbourhood.
Who are you going to call . . . ?'

Venkman joins in with an erratic off-key harmony:

'There's something wierd
And it don't look good . . .
Who are you going to call . . . ?'

And finally, lacking all rhythm or melody, Spengler adds his mournful baritone for the big finish as a flashbulb pops:

'Ghostbusters . .   Ghostbusters . . .!'

No one, it seems, can get away from them. Over toast, marmalade and coffee, Dana Barrett sits in her kitchen with the *New York Post* spread out on the counter-top. There they are. Slap-bang on the front page, under a banner headline reading, 'GHOST-BUSTERS?' – mouths hanging open as if caught in the act of singing.
Screwballs!
Dana shakes her head and turns to the review section. Over the radio comes the voice of Larry King, doing his phone-in talk show:
'And our phone-in topic today . . . Ghosts and Ghostbusting. The controversy builds as more sightings are reported, and some maintain that these pro-

fessional paranormal eliminators in New York are the cause of it all. Why did everything start just when these guys went into business? Should they be allowed to carry around unlicensed proton mass drivers? And what's wrong with ghosts anyway? Call us, all our lines are open . . . And our first call today . . . Hello, Larry King . . .'

A nasal female twang shrills through the ether.

'Hello, Larry? I think what Dr Spengler said in his interview with you yesterday was true . . . the world *is* in for a "psychic shock" as he put it, because like my aunt now, she reads coffee grounds, and she –'

Dana kills the radio with a vicious stab of her finger and flicks on the portable TV on the corner shelf.

The tanned, beefy mug of a breakfast-show host swims into view, surrounded by a jungle foliage of ferns and rubber plants.

'Are you saying that ghosts actually exist?' he's asking with bemused blue eyes and a condescending hint of a smile.

Dana groans and covers her eyes as a big close-up of Venkman's crumpled features fills the screen.

'Not only do they exist,' says Venkman earnestly, 'they're all over the place. And that's why we're offering this vitally important service to people in the whole Tri-State area.'

He smirks into camera and winds up for the hard sell.

'We're available twenty-four hours a day, seven days a week. We have the tools and we have the talent. No job is too big, no fee is too big. We're ready for anything!'

'Well, in any case,' the host chips in merrily, 'I

guess there's one big question on everybody's mind and you're certainly in a position to answer it for us. Have you seen Elvis and how is he?'

Dana grabs the marmalade jar and throws it with all her strength.

13

The alarm bell drills a hole through Stantz's be-
fuddled brain. He moans and pulls the bedclothes
over his head. But the alarm will not desist. Spengler
hauls at his shoulder and tumbles him out of bed.
Stantz staggers to his feet, and through a blur of utter
weariness and a cavernous yawn, fumbles his way to
the lockers.

Venkman, pale and bleary-eyed, with a three-day
stubble, is climbing into his jumpsuit. All three bump
and lurch against one another as they search for
leg-holes, tug zips, tighten straps.

Is this the tenth call in the past twenty-four hours,
Stantz wonders numbly, or the twenty-fourth in the
last ten? He's lost track of time and numbers these
past two weeks. Or is it three?

Suited-up, they fall against the brass pole and slide
into oblivion. Stantz closes his eyes dreamily, feeling
he could fall for ever. Until he's brought to his senses
with a bone-jarring jolt as his feet hit the floor.

Spengler, looking like death warmed up, is already
buckling on his proton pack and checking valence
readings to see that it's fully primed. Stantz grabs a
trap from the charger and clips it on to his belt.

74

Minutes later, moving like automatons, they pile into the Ectomobile and head off to the city, strobe lights flashing, siren wailing its mournful cry.

At the wheel, Stantz ponders sleepily for the umpteenth time just what the hell is going on. Two (three?) weeks ago there wasn't a reliable sighting of a ghost or ghoul in the Tri-State area. All of a sudden they're growing on trees. What was that Larry King said on his phone-in show the other day?

. . . some maintain that these professional paranormal eliminators are the cause of it all . . .?

Did that make sense? Was there any truth in it? If not – what precisely *was* causing this spate of sightings?

Stantz scratches his head and yawns. He's too tired to think straight. Leave it till tomorrow. Or the day after. Or next year.

Alone, Dana probably wouldn't have seen him. But coming out of the stage door of the Avery Fisher Hall after rehearsals, listening with half an ear to the grandiose opinions of the new young violinist, her eye roves in a distracted fashion over the open plaza in the middle of the Lincoln Center for the Performing Arts.

And there sits Venkman on the edge of the marble fountain, scruffily unkempt as ever, and looking as if he hasn't had a decent wink of sleep in a month.

In spite of herself, Dana gives a little private smile and her heart skips a semiquaver. But why on earth . . .? Doesn't she find the guy brash and pushy and objectionable?

Maybe.

But not as pretentious and predictable as the over-grown prodigy by her side. Excusing herself, Dana walks over, arranging her face carefully to convey an impression of cool politeness.

Venkman slides off the marble parapet. He's already noted the young man, tall and pale with a shock of fair hair, lingering in the background.

'Great rehearsal,' he greets her with a crooked smile.

Dana is surprised. 'You heard it?'

'You're the best one in your row.'

'Yeah?' Dana gives a sceptical twitch of an eyebrow. 'Most people can't hear just me with the whole orchestra playing. You're good.'

Venkman turns his back on the pale young man and strolls away, putting the fountain between them. 'I told you, the cello is my favourite instrument.'

'Really?' Dana says, scuffing her toe in a crack and trailing a little way behind. 'Do you have a favourite piece?'

Venkman stops with furrowed brow, sucking thoughtfully at his bottom lip. 'I'd have to say Prokofiev's Third Concerto,' he pronounces after due deliberation.

'That's a violin concerto.'

'Yeah, but it's got a great cello break.'

'Do you know what you're talking about?' Dana asks him with a faint edge of exasperation.

'I don't have to take abuse from you,' Venkman sniffs. 'I have other people dying to give it to me.'

'I know.' Dana smoothes the front of her Burberry raincoat. 'You're quite a celebrity these days.' She folds her arms and regards him shrewdly. 'So. Are you here because you have some information – about my case?'

Venkman looks at her. She has wonderful bones. He's mad about her chin. Her hair is a hazy tumbling cloud, a perfect frame for her wide eyes and clear brow. He wants to take her in his arms.

Instead he tilts his head and squints with one eye past her shoulder and says, 'Who's the stiff?'

Dana glances behind her to where the pale young man is inserting a nasal spray into each nostril. With an effort she tries not to laugh.

'The "stiff" happens to be one of the finest musicians in the world and a wonderful man,' she says stoutly.

'Is he dying or something?'

They both look at the pale young violinist, who chooses that moment to give each nostril a blast with the spray. 'He's a very close friend.'

She turns to Venkman once again.

'Do you have some explanation of what happened in my apartment?'

Venkman nods. 'Yes. But I have to tell you in private at a fine restaurant.'

'Can't you tell me now?'

'I'll cancel the reservation.' Venkman pulls a thick leather-bound book from his pocket. He holds it up for Dana to see. 'I found the name "Zuul" in the *Roylance Guide to Secret Societies and Sects*. I don't suppose you've read it.'

'You must have gotten the last copy.'

'Well,' Venkman goes on imperturbably, flipping the book open to a marked page. 'Apparently the name Zuul refers to a demi-god worshipped around 6000 BC by the . . .'

He bends closer, his eyes clouding. 'What's that say?' he asks, holding the book out.

'Hittites, the Mesopotamians and the Sumerians.'

Venkman watches her mouth as she reads: '"Zuul was the Minion of Gozer."'

'"Gozer,"' says Venkman with a thoughtful frown. 'He was very big in the Sumerian religion. One of their gods.

Dana looks at him curiously. 'What's he doing in my refrigerator?'

'I'm checking on that.' Venkman closes the book and slips it back into his pocket. 'I think we should meet Thursday night at nine to talk about it.'

'I don't think so,' Dana says firmly. 'I'm busy Thursday night.'

But Venkman won't be shaken. He says with an air of mild disgruntlement, 'You think I enjoy giving up my evenings to spend time with clients? I'm making an exception in your case because I respect you as an artist.' He tugs at her long knitted scarf. 'And as a dresser.'

Dana laughs. She considers for a moment and then makes up her mind.

'All right. Since you put it that way.'

'I'll pick you up at your place.'

Venkman taps his pocket and grins at her.

'I'll bring along the *Roylance Guide*. We can read after we eat.'

Dana nods. She still doesn't trust this bozo, but she can't help liking him. He doesn't seem to take the world or himself at all seriously, which she finds engaging and rather refreshing after the heavy high-brow company she's used to.

'I've got to go now.' She gives him a brief smile and walks back to the violinist, who for the past few minutes has been stamping his feet and giving Venkman the steely eye.

Venkman waves to him and calls out, 'You look very pale to me. I hope you get better soon.'

The violinist stands staring, hands thrust into the pockets of his overcoat. Dana covers her mouth

'Take good care of him,' Venkman shouts, and with arms daintily extended, twirls on his toes in a pretty pirouette round the empty plaza.

14

'Ghostbusters – please hold.'

Janine cancels the light and takes another call.

'Good afternoon, Ghostbusters – please hold.'

She switches back to the previous caller, ignoring the panel of winking lights and insistent beeps that haven't let up since she arrived in the office at nine this morning. This is getting ridiculous.

'Yes, can I help you?' Janine breaks her pencil point, searches for another pencil with one hand while she flips to a fresh page on the pad with the other.

She listens and nods, writing rapidly.

'Yes . . . yes . . . Is it just a mist or does it have arms and legs? Uh-huh . . . Well, the soonest we could possibly get to you would be a week from Friday . . .'

Janine sighs and raises her eyes to the large, powerfully-built black guy sitting over in the corner filling out a job application. He meets her look with a sympathetic shrug and goes back to the form.

'Well, I'm sorry, but we're completely booked until then . . . Uh-huh . . . Well, all I can suggest is that you stay out of your house until we can get to you. Thank you for calling . . .'

Janine handles the rest of the calls with the same brisk efficiency and then slumps back in her chair. Thankfully, for a few minutes at least, there is a respite.

Winston Zeddemore gets up and brings across the completed application form. He moves lightly and gracefully for such a big man, and stands gazing down at her with a pensive look that borders on the suspicious.

'Let me ask you something. The ad in the paper just said, "Help Wanted". What's the job?'

'I really don't know, Mr Zeddemore,' Janine apologises. 'They just told me to take applications and ask you these questions.'

She picks up a sheet of paper and adjusts her glasses and starts to read out the list of questions in a flat Brooklyn monotone:

'Do you believe in UFOs, astral projection, mental telepathy, ESP, clairvoyance, spirit photography, full-trance mediums, telekinetic movement, black and/or white magic, pyramidology, the theory of Atlantis, the Loch Ness Monster, or in general in spooks, spectres, wraiths, geists and ghosts?'

She looks up at him as Winston mulls it over with a thoughtful crease across his broad black forehead. Finally, he says, 'Not really. However, if there's a semi-regular pay cheque in it I'll believe anything you say.'

Stantz swings the Ectomobile into the garage bay and cuts the engine. He slides out from behind the wheel, slowly straightens up as if his bones might snap, and flexes his shoulders. Venkman climbs wearily out the other side, dangling three traps at arm's length.

A miasma of pungent green fumes surrounds their now blackened and dented metallic casings. The valence indicators flash red, confirming that our heroes have recently had close encounters of the spiritual kind. Nasty little babies they were too.

Which is plainly evident from the state of Venkman and Stantz.

Visors and jumpsuits covered in jellylike slime. Particle throwers seared at the nozzles. Faces strained and taut with battle fatigue.

And the Ectomobile looking like it's been through a major war and only made it by the skin of its bumpers.

Stantz slips off his proton pack and groans with relief. He wipes a mixture of sweat and slime from his forehead. 'Boy, that was a rough one.'

Venkman drops the traps into a large metal container with a hinged lid, temporary storage before they're sealed away in the main ecto-chamber in the basement. 'I can't take much more of this,' he complains in a ragged voice. 'The pace is killing me.'

Together they plod upstairs to the office.

Passing through on his way to the rear office, Venkman drops a paper on Janine's desk. 'Here's the invoice on the Brooklyn job. She paid with a Visa card.'

Janine takes it and impales it on a spike, and hands a thick sheaf of work orders to Stantz. 'Here are tonight's calls.'

Stantz riffles through them listlessly.

'Oh, no. Two more free-roaming repeaters.'

'And this is Winston Zeddemore. He came about the job.'

Stantz sticks out his hand. 'Ray Stantz. Pete Venkman. You're hired.'

'And someone from the EPA is here to see you,' Janine informs Venkman.

He pauses with one hand on the gate and frowns over his shoulder at her. 'The Environmental Protection Agency? What's he want?'

'I didn't ask him,' says Janine shortly. 'All I know is that I haven't had a break in two weeks and you promised you'd hire more help.'

'Janine,' Venkman says gently, 'I'm sure a woman with your qualifications would have no trouble finding a top-flight job in the housekeeping or food service industries.'

'Oh, really?' Janine retorts to his retreating back. 'Well, I've quit better jobs than this one, believe me!'

The panel lights up and she hits the switch with a lethal swipe.

On their way downstairs to the basement storage facility, Stantz glances through Winston's job application. He gives a low appreciative whistle.

'Very impressive résumé. "Electronic countermeasures . . . Strategic Air Command . . . Black belt in karate . . . small arms expert."' Stantz eyes him keenly. 'Mr Zeddemore, as you may have heard, we locate ghosts and spirits, trap them with streams of concentrated quantum energy, and remove them from people's homes, offices and places of worship . . .'

'Yeah, I heard that,' Winston says blandly, noting the proton mass drivers hung on their racks. 'Now tell me what you really do.'

15

The man from the EPA has his narrow pointed nose up against the press-cutting board when Venkman arrives. The office is plastered with newspaper and magazine items, in half-a-dozen different languages. Already he's skimmed through the *Newsweek* article and is nosing his way through the Bernstein piece in the *Washington Post*.

Venkman smells trouble. He's tired and he doesn't like the back of the EPA man's thin white neck. He doesn't like the EPA man's tightly-fitting check suit. And when the EPA man turns, he likes even less his prim ginger beard, watery blue eyes, and hard lipless mouth, like an appendectomy scar.

So he's cool, polite, watchful, as he comes round the desk and flops into his chair.

'Can I help you?'

'I'm Walter Peck. I represent the Environmental Protection Agency, Third District.'

He shoots his cuff and extends a skinny clawlike hand. Venkman waves his fingers. 'Great!' he says with a terrific lack of enthusiasm. 'How's it going?'

Peck wanders round the office, poking into corners and scanning files and correspondence in wire trays.

'Are you Peter Venkman?'

'I'm *Doctor* Venkman.'

Peck glances out of the corner of his eye at Venkman's pale, exhausted face, at his soiled jumpsuit stained with ectoplasmic residue, and says with a snide, patronising half-smile:

'Exactly what are you a doctor of, Mr Venkman?'

'I have Ph.D.s in Psychology and Parapsychology.'

'I see.' Without being invited, Peck sits down in the chair opposite, and fussily crosses his legs. 'And now you catch ghosts?' he says with his snide, twisted smile.

The question contains a veiled insinuation, which Venkman chooses to ignore.

'You could say that.'

'And how many ghosts have you caught, Mr Venkman?'

'I'm not at liberty to say.'

Peck's watery blue gaze drifts round the office, taking it in, summing it up, writing it off. His narrow mouth tightens and his gaze hardens as he switches his attention to Venkman once more.

'And where do you put these ghosts once you catch them?'

'In a storage facility,' says Venkman stolidly. A pulse starts to throb in his temple. With great effort he breathes in and breathes out, slowly and calmly.

Peck persists.

'And would this storage facility be located on these premises?'

'Yes, it would.'

'And may I see this storage facility?'

'No,' says Venkman quietly. 'You may not.'

'And why not, Mr Venkman?'

'Because you didn't say the magic word,' Venkman tells him in a gentle, flippant tone, which has something dangerous lurking beneath it. Like a tarantula disturbed from peaceful slumber underneath a warm rock.

Peck sighs. He looks pained.

'And what *is* the magic word, Mr Venkman?'

'The magic word is "please",' Venkman says, unsmiling.

Peck gives a little nervous cough and the side of his face twitches in a weak grin. He scratches his ginger beard and opens his eyes a fraction wider. 'May I *please* see the storage facility?'

'*Why* do you want to see it?'

'Well, because I'm curious,' Peck says, suddenly thrusting his thin white neck forward and fixing Venkman with his watery blue stare. 'I want to know more about what you do here. Frankly, there have been a lot of wild stories in the media, and we want to assess any possible environmental impact from your operation –'

The pulse in Venkman's temple is visible now. A hard, ugly lump of anger is forcing its way up inside his gut. His tiredness has given way to a cold and clinical and implacable rage.

And still the man from the EPA goes remorselessly on.

'– For instance, the storage of noxious, possibly hazardous waste materials in your basement. Now either you show me what's down there or I come back with a court order.'

He sits back with a thin self-satisfied smirk. His duty has been properly discharged. The ultimatum delivered. The weight and force of officialdom is on his side. There only remains the final victory of capitulation.

But Venkman doesn't like ultimatums and he'll be damned if he's going to give in to this thin-necked, watery-eyed, ginger-bearded bureaucrat pipsqueak. Never. Not in a million years.

He stands. Places his knuckles on the desk. Leans menacingly across and gives it to Peck full in the face.

'Go ahead! Get a court order! Then I'm gonna sue your ass off for wrongful prosecution!'

Peck flushes. He buttons his jacket, grabs his briefcase, and marches stiff-legged to the door.

'Have it your way, Mr Venkman,' he says in a tight, strangulated voice, and barges blindly out.

'Hey!' Venkman shouts after him. 'Make yourself useful! Go save a tree!'

And swings round and kicks the wastepaper basket clear across the room.

16

Meanwhile, in the basement, Winston Zeddemore is having problems with his credibility quotient.

His goggling eyes tell him that these guys are for real, while his bruised and battered brain refuses to accept the message. What knocks him through the loop is the casual, quite matter-of-fact way Stantz and his egghead chum, Spengler, go about their ghostly trade. As if trapping spooks and containing them with laser beams behind a wall of concrete blocks in the basement were the most natural supernatural thing in the world.

Spengler shakes his hand and smiles a greeting in a vague, abstracted way, and goes back to tinkering with a damaged proton pack on the littered workbench. He reaches for a soldering iron and bends his beaky nose to the task with an intense, lugubrious concentration.

Stantz calls Winston across and starts to explain how the storage facility operates. In one hand he holds a steaming ecto-trap, while with the other he yanks a steel lever down.

'Set entry grid.'

There is the oiled whine of internal hydraulics,

followed by a solid mechanical clunk. In the wall of concrete blocks, reaching from floor to ceiling, a small hatch – as thick and substantial as the door of a safe – has slid open, revealing a rectangular boxlike slit.

Winston watches with a kind of mesmerised disbelief as Stantz inserts the trap into the slit and activates the lever, shutting the heavy steel hatch. He presses a couple of buttons.

'Lock entry grid. Neutronise laser-containment system.'

Winston cocks his head and listens. From within comes a crackling and snapping, like the sound of bugs being fried on an outdoor insect light. Then a deep electronic burp. Then silence.

Stantz repeats the procedure, opens the hatch, removes the trap, and tosses it into a bin marked: FOR RECHARGE.

He holds up his empty hands, like a magician finishing a clever disappearing trick, his round face splitting into a cheerful grin.

'That's all there is to it.'

Winston nods weakly, bereft of speech. Stantz gestures him over to a hooded viewing port and jerks his thumb. Winston decides to humour him and peers in through the smoked glass screen, about the size of a small TV monitor.

If he ever needed a graphic depiction of hell, this is it.

A yellow graveyard mist hangs in thick streamers. Spectral shapes, looking lost and lonely, waft aimlessly to and fro. Vaguely human forms stand desolate, staring into eternity. Strange lights flicker and die, creating an eerie, unearthly twilight, and dimly illuminating this bleak limbo of lost souls and despairing spooks.

Winston pulls away and wipes the icy perspiration from the back of his muscular neck with a trembling hand. Jesus. These guys aren't fooling. The stories in the paper are true.

'I've got to sleep,' Spengler groans, throwing a screwdriver on to the workbench. He pushes up his glasses and massages his eyes, stifling a yawn.

'I need two new purge valves,' Stantz informs him. 'How's the laser-containment grid holding up?'

Spengler casts a doubtful glance at the storage facility and shakes his head.

'I'm worried, Ray. It's getting crowded in there. And all my recent data points to something big on the bottom.'

'What do you mean – "big"?' Winston says, blinking.

Spengler picks up a candy bar from the workbench and holds it up thoughtfully. 'Well, let's say this Twinkie represents the *normal* amount of psychokinetic energy in the New York area at any given time. According to this morning's PKE sample, the current level in the city would be a Twinkie thirty-five-feet long, weighing approximately 600 pounds.'

Winston purses his lips. 'That's a big Twinkie.'

Stantz's eyes flick from Spengler to the concrete wall and back again. He rubs his chin and says gravely, 'We could be on the verge of a fourfold crossover . . . or worse. If what we're seeing indicates a massive PKE surge, we could experience an actual rip . . .'

He looks round as Venkman comes down the stairs.

Venkman doesn't look happy. He looks like he's got a ton of trouble on either shoulder. He gnaws his lip and says:

'Egon, how's the laser-containment grid holding up?'

In answer, Spengler shakes his head. Stantz says, 'It's not good, Pete.'

Winston says, 'Tell him about the Twinkie.'

Venkman crosses to the viewing port but can't bring himself to peek inside. He leans against the wall, grey in the face. The others wait in silence.

Venkman says, 'We've got another problem,' and starts to tell them about the prick from the EPA.

17

A menacing Manhattan night.

A full moon rides fitfully through scudding banks of dark cloud. Shadows pass like wraiths over the towers of steel and glass, and deepen the gloom of the concrete canyons.

A deeper, darker shadow moves over the upper west side of the city and gathers itself above the high-rise apartment building located at 78th and Central Park West.

There it hovers and thickens, winding about itself in tortuous blue-black coils. There is something almost sentient about it, as if it contained a presence with a brain and a pair of eyes and a purpose. And as if that purpose was soon to be realised, brought at last to ultimate fulfilment.

At the pinnacle of the building, a dull pulsating glow begins to emanate from the polished dome of the temple.

Casting an eerie, shifting light over the bronze doors, the marble pillars, the pale stone balustrades.

Throwing into stark, grotesque relief the pair of huge carved beasts rampant, on their plinths. With paws raised, lips drawn back in frozen stone snarls, they resemble the mythical hounds of hell.

The glow bathes these hideous horned creatures
. . . and it might be a trick of the shifting light that
there is a tiny, barely perceptible movement –

But no, not possible. They are made of stone.

Dead stone.

A few grains of dust sift down from the raised paw
of one of the creatures. A fine, hairline crack appears.
The solid dead stone seems to tremble. And all at
once there is the clearly audible sound of cracking
and creaking as the stone crumbles away to reveal
the black curled claws, sharp as talons.

The claws twitch in spasm and slowly flex.

The fissure in the stone spreads along the paw.
Fragments pulverise and fall to the floor. Then whole
massive chunks as the horned beast, the mythical
creature – the Terror Dog – comes slowly and creak-
ingly to life.

Its dead stone eye blinks open.

It is a huge baleful eye.

With slitted pupil.

Glowing red.

Evil.

As the elevator doors slide open, Dana hears the
blast of music from Louis's apartment. The night of
the party. Since Louis mentioned it, she hasn't given
it another thought.

Dana glides quickly and quietly along the hallway
with a light tread. With any luck Louis will be too
engrossed with his guests to be on the lookout for
her – and besides, he won't be able to hear a thing
with all that dreadful racket going on.

Luck isn't on her side. Either that or Louis has a Dana Barrett detector grafted on to his cerebral cortex.

For she hasn't gone two paces past his apartment when the door is flung open and Louis rushes out. His thin face is flushed and excited, his beady close-set eyes lighting up as he spies Dana creeping along the corridor.

'Oh, Dana – it's you!' Louis exclaims, with a pathetic attempt at surprise. He wears a silk shirt slashed with garish colours and a gilt medallion on his chest, which don't go at all well with his grey baggy wide-bottomed trousers and tan lace-up shoes.

Dana halts in mid-creep, and with an effort conjures up a smile from somewhere.

'Hi, Louis.'

'Hey, it's crazy in here!' Louis scuttles over, rubbing his hands. He beams up at her hopefully. 'You're missing a classic party.'

Dana hesitates. 'Well . . . actually, Louis, I have a friend coming by . . .'

'Great!' Louis flutters his hands in the air. 'Bring her along.' A frown corrugates his narrow forehead as he warns, 'But you better hurry. I made nachos with non-fat cheese and they're almost gone.' He smiles generously. 'I'll make some more though.'

'Fine, Louis.' He follows Dana to the door of her apartment and watches as she lets herself in. She smiles at him through the crack. 'We'll stop by for a drink.'

'I got a Twister game for later –' Louis says, but finds he's talking to the closed door. He trails back to his own apartment and finds another closed door.

'Hey, lemme in!' Louis yells, pounding on the door.

But the music drowns both his cries and the sound of his puny fists, and Louis has to keep on pounding to be let in to his own party.

From the wide windows, the sky over the park is dark with purple thunderclouds. In the distance, beyond the East River, forked lightning flickers briefly like a serpent's tongue. The storm is gathering and heading this way, Dana judges.

The apartment is oppressively warm. She dumps her Nike holdall by the bedroom door and tosses her coat over the back of a chair. Underneath she is wearing a figure-hugging blue leotard and thick woollen leg-warmers. Strands of curly hair adhere damply to her forehead.

Dana switches on the table-lamp and sinks slowly back into her favourite armchair, closing her eyes with a deep, luxurious sigh of contentment. The dance work-out was great; this is even better. Relax: shower: dress. Plenty of time before Venkman arrives with his – what was it now? – *Roylance Guide to Secret Societies and Sects*. Dana smiles sleepily to herself.

It is very quiet.

Hum of traffic on Central Park West. Distant, almost soothing rumble of thunder somewhere over Queens. Dana tries to decide what to wear but a torpid drowsiness weighs heavily on her limbs and eyelids. She drifts down and down into bottomless space . . .

The jangle of the phone jerks her awake, eyes

"Ghostbusters" – ready to save the world

left: Dana and Louis – Gate-keeper and Keymaster

above: Gozer, high on "Spook Central" – with the fearsome "Terror Dog"

right: Dr. Venkman visits Dana in her apartment

left: The first fully func-
tional "Ectomobile"
in the world, leaves
"Ghostbusters" H.Q.

right: Dr. Raymond

Devastation in the city – you better call, "Ghostbusters"

"Ghostbusters" in action – crossing the streams!

blinking wide. Cursing under her breath, Dana
cradles the receiver against her shoulder.

'Hello . . . Oh, hi Mom. Yes . . . yes, everything's
fine. No, nothing. Just that one time . . .'

Dana listens to the tinny rattle of the voice, nodding
her head.

'I am . . . I will . . . I won't. Mother! I'm all right,
I told you. Everything's fine now . . . Yes!' She listens
patiently some more. 'All right. Good. I'll talk to
you tomorrow. I promise. 'Bye.'

She hangs up and slumps back, eyes closed. The
pool of lamplight cascades over her slender reclining
form, her tousled head, her chest rhythmically rising
and falling. The rest of the room is in deep shadow.
Dana sleeps.

In the narrow slit beneath the kitchen door, a light
begins to glow.

It grows in intensity. It becomes brighter, and
brighter still, filtering through the cracks round the
door and sending wafer-thin shafts of brilliant white
light lancing into the shadowy room like tiny search-
light beams.

A thin white beam falls across Dana's closed eyelids. She frowns in her sleep and stirs uneasily. Opens
her eyes and looks muzzily towards the kitchen door.

Then Dana is starkly, chillingly wide-awake.

'Oh, shit!'

She stares at the dark rectangle of the door, framed
in streaming phosphorescent light. And even as she
watches, the door itself is suffused with a molten
crimson glow. Transformed into a fluid shimmering
membrane the colour of hellfire.

Dana gasps aloud as the imprint of sharp curved claws appears, seeking to tear their way through the membrane with demonic force and fury. And the door is bending now, buckling under the onslaught of the tearing claws.

All the strength seems to have seeped out of Dana's bones.

With a tremendous effort she grips the arms of the chair and levers herself forward, and as she does so a black, scaly, inhuman hand rips through the cushion behind her and clutches her breast.

The cushion rips again and another clawlike hand tears through the upholstery and encircles her waist.

Dana screams. She bucks wildly in the chair, seeking to pull the black clawlike hands from her body. Again the cushion rips and another hand encloses her neck in its scaly grip, while yet another rips through and clamps itself across her mouth.

The armchair swings round to face the kitchen door. It starts to move, gathering pace. Dana's eyes widen in mute horror as she is propelled forward, pinned to the chair and gagged by the powerful clutching hands.

The molten crimson door bulges outwards. And suddenly explodes as if sucked off its hinges by a hurricane wind. Beyond is where the kitchen used to be.

Now a vast fiery cavern, flickering and fragmenting in the tremendous heat. Dana feels its scorching blast as the chair gathers speed and races towards it. And deep within the inferno, she glimpses the most terrible sight of all.

Two pairs of glowing, blood-red eyes.

The Terror Dogs.

Lifting their huge black snouts, the hanging flesh round their slavering jaws crinkles in what seems to be almost a smiling snarl of welcome. Their paws are raised, their viciously pointed claws, glinting redly, outstretched towards her.

Then the chair, the clutching hands, and Dana, disappear through the doorway and are swallowed up in the fiery depths of the chamber.

The storm is here at last. Racing in from the east, the dark tumbling clouds mass over the city. A flash of lightning streaks jaggedly across the sky. Thunder rolls over the temple dome.

The bronze doors reflect the lightning in dull flickering gleams. It illuminates the tall fluted pillars and stone balustrades and the broad flight of steps.

It also illuminates the empty stone pedestals, now strewn with fragments of pulverised rock, where the creatures once stood.

Once. No longer.

18

'Do you have any Excedrin or Extra Strength Tylenol?' the tall woman in the shiny green dress with the sequinned cleavage screams in Louis's ear.

They are standing in Louis's cramped kitchenette, in a tiny alcove off the living-room. The apartment has none of the spaciousness of Dana's apartment, nor its spectacular view, overlooking as it does a dank brick lightwell in the centre of the building.

From his windows, during daylight hours, Louis has the totally exclusive privilege of watching people going about their business in the bathroom opposite, and occasionally, to break the monotony, pigeons doing their dirt on the air-conditioning duct.

Louis strains up on tiptoe to hear what the tall woman is saying. A throbbing disco beat vibrates the molecules in the air to a frenzy, drowning out all human communication.

Couples and trios sit in isolation in corners of the room, attempting to lip-read. A middle-aged man shaped like a peardrop is browsing through a tattered magazine, as if whiling away the time in a dentist's waiting-room. Someone is going round with a Windex cloth, emptying and cleaning the already empty and clean ashtrays.

And this is the high point of the evening.

'I have acetacylasilic acid, but the generic brand from Walgreens,' Louis yells back at the tall woman, having finally understood her request. ''Cause I can get 600 tablets for thirty-five per cent less than the cost of 300 tablets name brand. Is it a headache?' he shrills at her, his voice breaking with the strain.

But the tall woman in the green dress has drifted off across the room and is peering wistfully into the tropical fish tank as if she might be tempted to dive in and join them.

Louis is having a wonderful time. What would make it really perfect was if Dana was here. He hopes she'll come and bring her friend. They're short of two women to even out the numbers.

He waves to a young man with a wispy beard and thick pebble glasses who's trying to read the fire regulations behind the door, and discos his way across to the buffet table, clicking his fingers above his head.

Two men in stiff suits are helping themselves to the lavish spread. One wears a loose spotted bow tie, dangling down slightly so that the elastic shows, the other a see-through yellow nylon shirt with a Disneyworld motif visible underneath.

The man with the bow tie is about to bite into a canapé when Louis points at it, so that the man nearly has Louis's finger in his mouth.

Louis leans forward and shouts above the din.

'That's Nova Scotia salmon. The real thing. It costs $24.95 a pound but really $12.48 a pound net after tax.' He flings his arm out. 'I'm writing this whole party off as a promotional expense. That's why I invited clients instead of friends. Try that Brie. It's dynamite at room temperature.'

A thought strikes him and he glances round. 'Maybe I should turn the heat up a bit . . .'

A blonde buxom girl in a frilly pink dress tugs plaintively at Louis's arm. Two white lines run through her suntan over her bare shoulders and down her back.

'C'mon, then,' he pleads. 'Maybe if we dance other people will start.'

They take to the empty floor just as the doorbell rings.

Louis excuses himself and rushes to the door, expecting, hoping it's Dana. It isn't. It's a young couple going on forty-five. Louis takes their coats and leads them through to the hotbed of activity in the living-room.

'Everybody – this is Ted and Annette Fleming. Ted has a small carpet-cleaning business in receivership, but Annette is drawing a salary from a deferred bonus from two years ago and the house has $15,000 left at eight per cent . . .'

He leaves them to it and detours through to the bedroom to dump the coats.

Louis pushes open the door and tosses the coats on to the bed. On the bed, several feet high, with a head the size of a lion's, stands a Terror Dog. Saliva leaks from its gaping jaws. Its pointed fangs gleam in the light from the living-room.

Monstrous claws splayed out, it stands four-square, looking at Louis with saucer-sized red eyes, the pupils black and slitted.

Until the coats land on its head, carelessly thrown by the unheeding and unsuspecting Louis, who closes the door and returns to the party, humming a happy little tune.

The roar from the bedroom shakes the plaster off the ceiling and locks all the guests in an instant freeze-frame.

Canapés remain unchewed, words cut off in midair, gestures turned into stiff waxworks. Everyone stares at Louis as he stands there glowering at them, hands on hips. Louis is not pleased.

'Okay. Who brought the dog?'

The bedroom door disintegrates in a shower of splinters and sheared timber.

Like a lumbering rhino, the Terror Dog smashes straight through it with such force that it skids halfway across the room, ripping the carpet into shreds.

Leaping in all directions, the screaming guests scramble frantically away from the snarling beast. It whips its thickly-muscled neck round, glowing red eyes as big as headlamps scanning the room for something or someone.

Someone.

Louis Tully.

With his back flattened against the wall, Louis slithers towards the apartment door. The Terror Dog turns and fixes its eyes upon him. Its jaws gape in a snarling grin. A growl from the pit of its stomach shakes the foundations of the building. Its haunches bunch as it prepares to leap.

Louis leaps first – gets to the door, wrenches it open, dives into the corridor, slams the door behind him.

Not a split-second too soon as the Terror Dog gives the door the same treatment and smashes it to smithereens.

By now Louis is halfway along the corridor, putting up a time for the hundred metres that Carl Lewis wouldn't sniff at. The elevator doors yawn open. As the beast charges towards him, Louis desperately hits the button with his fist and the doors slide shut.

The doorman touches the peak of his cap as the cab pulls away from the kerb and returns to his station outside the revolving doors.

Face white and streaked with perspiration, Louis bounds out of the building, screaming at the top of his voice, 'Help! Help! There's a bear loose in my apartment!' and without stopping dashes through the traffic and leaps over the wall across the street.

'Now he's got animals up there,' the doorman mutters to himself, and stands shaking his head, watching Louis, shirt-tails flapping, vanish into the dark undergrowth of Central Park.

The Terror Dog hits the doorman square between the shoulderblades, knocking him flat. In two gigantic leaps, the snarling horned beast is across the street and over the wall and out of sight.

The chase has only just begun.

19

Louis runs for his life. He has no idea where he's heading, and really doesn't care. Just as long as that – thing doesn't get hold of him.

He stumbles on through the park, tripping over roots and getting swiped by branches. He comes to a dark concrete underpass and staggers into it, his footsteps echoing and hollow. Ahead he sees a fairytale twinkle of lights, and realises it's the swank Central Park restaurant, Tavern on the Green. Louis has never eaten there, can't afford to, though he knows the place by repute.

The wide picture windows pour forth a blaze of golden light on to the asphalt courtyard.

Inside, the élite of New York are dining in an atmosphere of elegant refinement, the superb food and wines complemented by the muted chords of a grand piano over in the corner. Lithe waiters in tails swivel to and fro, bearing silver dishes.

Gasping and choking, Louis limps up to the windows and searches for a door. Thankfully, he sees one and tugs at the handle. It is locked. He runs along the side of the building, turns a corner and finds another door Also locked.

This is getting serious. Possibly terminal.

Panicking now, he presses his face to the glass and tries frantically to attract someone's attention. Everybody is too busy having a good time to notice.

Louis spins round as a rustling of leaves and snapping of twigs comes from the bushes. It sounds like something large and very heavy moving closer through the undergrowth.

Then he hears it.

A throaty grumbling growl.

Then he sees it.

A single, black-slitted, glowing red eye watching him through the bushes.

Louis falls back, spread-eagled against the blazing light of the wide picture window. He turns and hammers with his fists on the glass, his face contorted into a grimace of abject terror. The elegant diners look up, hearing the muffled cries for help above the tinkling piano, and return to their Trout Vinaigrette and Tangerine Mousse.

A horned shadow falls across the paved courtyard. Louis stands paralysed with fear as the black lumbering form of the Terror Dog advances towards him out of the bushes. There is water in his veins and jelly in his knees. He extends a thin trembling hand and coos in a hoarse cracked whisper:

'Nice doggie . . . Nice . . .'

The beast snarls. Roars. And pounces.

For just a moment the subdued chatter inside the Tavern on the Green ceases as everyone listens to the savage roar from outside, followed by a violent threshing and a pitifully plaintive cry, followed by silence.

The polite chatter resumes.

Louis walks out of the park into Columbus Circle. He turns sharp right in the middle of the pavement and walks stiffly to a line of horse-and-carriages at the kerbside. He turns sharp left and approaches the horse at the head of the line. He goes up to the horse and stands next to it. He speaks to the horse.

His voice is calm. Emotionless. Quite dead.

Staring into space, he chants:

'I am Vinz Clortho. Keymaster of Gozer. Volguus Zildrohar. Lord of the Sebouillia. Are you the Gate-keeper?'

The horse looks at him but doesn't reply.

The coachman in flat peaked cap and cape calls down from his seat:

'Hey, buddy! He pulls the wagon. I make the deals. You wanna ride?'

Louis turns his head mechanically and addresses the coachman.

'Are you the Gatekeeper?'

'Naw, I'm the Governor of New Jersey.' The coach-man curls his lip. 'Now get outta here.'

Louis fixes his eyes on the coachman. The eyes begin to glow a deep dull red. The pupils are black and slitted. Louis raises his arm and points directly at the coachman. His voice rings with a dreadful avenging doom.

'You will perish in flames, subcreature! Gozer will destroy you and your kind!'

Louis turns woodenly to the horse and whispers:

107

'Wait for the sign. Then all prisoners will be released.'

Without waiting for an answer, he marches stiffly into the several lanes of traffic speeding round Columbus Circle. Cars screech and swerve. Horns blare.

The noise and disruption alerts two mounted policemen eating frankfurters outside a hot-dog stand. They exchange glances, and wheeling their horses about, set off at a slow trot to follow Louis's somnambulistic progress down Broadway.

20

Stantz is bushed. He sprawls back in the passenger seat of the Ectomobile, head lolling from side to side as Winston steers the big car along the Hudson Parkway.

To their right, the river is a solid dark band, and beyond, the lights of the New Jersey shoreline sparkle brightly in the overcast evening light. It's been an odd sort of day, Stantz reflects. The storm that's been threatening all afternoon seems to be hanging directly over the city, yet refuses to break. As if, he thinks, his tired mind fantasising, it's waiting for something . . .

And that last job was pretty peculiar too. Stantz mulls over the memory, reliving it pleasurably in his mind.

They'd been called out on an assignment at, of all places, the single officers' quarters at Fort Detmerring. He and Winston had taken the call. So they'd raced up there, strobe lights on, siren blaring, the whole works, and set about tracking down the spook that was said to be haunting the barracks.

While Winston checked the basement, Stantz had investigated the officers' sleeping quarters. Pretty

impressive they were, too. One room had been pains-
takingly restored with period furniture, mirrors,
drapes, even a four-poster bed.

Fascinated, Stantz had poked around with his PKE
meter, but hadn't come up with anything. He checked
out the large ornate wardrobe, packed with dress
uniforms and sabres in racks, and still no sign of
anything in the least paranormal. Stantz shook his
head and gave the room a final once-over.

The four-poster bed looked wide and soft and very
inviting.

He tested his weight on it, squeezing the thick
sprung mattress. Then unbuckled his harness and laid
the proton pack on the carpet. Slipped out of his
soiled jumpsuit and stretched out on the bed, wrig-
gling his toes.

Bliss.

He closed his eyes and instantly fell asleep.

It was the next bit he wasn't sure about. Whether
he was awake or dreaming, experiencing reality or
subconscious fantasy.

Anyway, this pink mist started to form on the
ceiling. At first it was swirling, shapeless, and he
could remember quite distinctly watching it slither
slowly downwards and seep through the heavy bro-
cade canopy over the bed.

Then it began to change, alter shape, assume the
form of a long vaporous shroud hanging over the
entire length of his body. In his dream – reality? –
Stantz wasn't in the least frightened or alarmed. He
simply lay watching the pink apparition hovering
inches above his face.

And the pair of beautiful eyes looking into his

They belonged to a lovely haunted creature, a lost soul perhaps, with a voluptuous body that was forming and defining itself even as he watched.

Stantz held his breath as this vision pressed closer upon him. For a moment he thought he might be smothered. But the ghostly, beautiful face slid down his body out of sight. Then curled round into a puff of pink mist and evaporated into thin air.

Stantz propped himself up on his elbows. His emotions were mixed, perplexity and disappointment in equal measure. But *something* was there. He could feel it. His throat went dry and tight. He couldn't get his breath properly. He stared.

The leather tongue of his belt was sliding out of the buckle. His belt came undone. The fastener on his pants opened. His zip began to slide down.

Unable to move, Stantz watched all this happening with a kind of stupefied amazement. He didn't know whether or not he ought to be scared. He decided he wasn't scared. Quite the opposite, in fact.

He was actually starting to enjoy it. Very much.

Stantz lay back on the bed and closed his eyes. He breathed a sigh through his nose. You might win some, he thought with a smile on his lips, but you couldn't win them all.

'Do you believe in God, Ray?'

Stantz jerks out of his dreaming reverie and sits up, blinking. They've turned off the Parkway and are passing the Cathedral on Amsterdam Avenue. He lights a cigarette and pops open a can of beer.

'No, but I think Jesus had style.'

'I believe,' Winston says. He means it. His face in

the light of the dashboard is sombre and deep in thought.

Stantz gives a slight shrug and drinks his beer. Whatever people choose to believe is okay with him. 'Parts of the Bible are great,' he says agreeably.

Winston nods to himself. Several moments pass, and then he says, 'Ray, do you remember something in the Bible about a day when the dead would rise up from their graves?'

'And the seas would boil . . .' Stantz says, yawning. He takes another swig and tries to dredge his memory for where that came from.

'Right. And the sky would fall.'

Stantz remembers. 'Revelations: "And after three days and an half the Spirit of life from God entered into them, and they stood upon their feet; and great fear fell upon them which saw them." Judgment Day.'

'Yeah, Judgment Day,' says Winston thoughtfully.

'Every ancient religion had its own myth about the end of the world.'

Winston is staring through the windscreen, gripping the wheel with both hands.

'Has it ever occurred to you, Ray, that the reason we've been so busy lately is because the dead have been rising from their graves?'

Stantz lowers his can of beer and slowly turns his head to look at Winston. He belches. The taste is sour on his tongue.

21

A man in a doorman's uniform with a badly bruised
face is being helped into an ambulance when Venkman arrives outside Dana's building. Two cops are
holding back a small crowd of curious bystanders.

For once Venkman looks presentable in a neat
dark suit, with a collar and tie. His shoes are polished.
He is carrying a bunch of flowers. He pauses before
pushing through the revolving door and asks one of
the cops what's going on.

'Some moron brought a cougar to a party and it
went berserk,' he is informed.

'Oh.'

Venkman crosses the lobby and steps into the
elevator. He gets out at the thirty-fifth floor and walks
along the corridor. The splintered remains of a door
are scattered over the green carpet. Venkman looks
at them pensively for a second, and then carries on
to Dana's apartment.

He rings the bell, and when there is no answer,
rings again and knocks. 'Dana?'

The door swings open very slowly and Dana – or
somebody resembling Dana – is revealed.

Venkman stands and gazes at this new Dana. Her

eyes are large and dark and lustrous in a white, drawn face. Her full lips are wet and parted. Her tumbled cloud of hair hangs down loosely on to her pale naked shoulders. Most of her breasts are visible above the thin silk shift of flaming crimson that follows every curve and crevice of her body.

He can hear the breath whispering in her distended nostrils, quivering with passionate sensuality.

Venkman nods pleasantly. 'Hi. That's a different look for you, isn't it?'

The woman Dana looks at him as if at a stranger. She raises her head imperiously and says in a throaty whisper:

'Are you the Keymaster?'

'Not that I know of.'

The door shuts. Venkman knocks again. The door opens.

'Are you the Keymaster?'

'Yes,' Venkman says, and slips inside before she can change her mind.

Dana stands facing him, shoulders held back, chin lifted haughtily. There is a blankness, a deadness, about her eyes.

'I am Zuul,' she announces. 'I am the Gatekeeper.'

Cosy, thinks Venkman. Keymaster. Gatekeeper. They should get on like a house on fire.

Speaking of fires, he notices for the first time the state of the apartment. The kitchen door is missing and the door-frame is charred and blackened with soot. One of the armchairs has gaping holes right through the upholstery, the springs sticking out.

Venkman drops the flowers into a wastebasket and

takes her by the elbow. 'Come on, I think we better get out of here.'

Dana pulls away from him and crosses quickly to the window. Her eyes narrow as she searches the sky. Her breasts rise and fall voluptuously.

'No – we must prepare for the coming of Gozer.'

'Okay, I'll help,' Venkman offers, under the circumstances thinking it wise to humour her. 'Should we make some dip or something?'

Dana turns to face him, her eyes huge and round, darkly luminescent. 'He is the Destructor.'

'Really. Can't wait to meet him.'

Dana holds out both arms to him. Venkman takes her hands in his, wondering what next. What next is that she leads him swiftly and silently into the bedroom and lays down full-length on the bed.

'Do you want this body?' Dana asks brazenly, the breath rasping in her throat. Her hands grasp him fiercely and draw him down to lie on top of her.

'Is that a trick question?' Venkman asks, extricating himself from her powerful grip. He lifts her wrist and checks her pulse.

'Take me now!' Dana implores him.

Venkman unclips a pencil spotlight from his pocket and leans over to examine her pupil dilation.

'I make it a rule never to sleep with possessed people.'

Her arm snakes round his neck and she drags him down on top of her. Her lips fasten on his with supernatural lust.

Venkman surfaces and draws breath. 'Actually,' he pants, 'it's more of a guideline than a rule.'

Dana holds his head in the palms of her hands, her long nails digging into his cheekbones.

'I want you inside me.'

'I don't know,' Venkman says uncertainly. 'You've got two people in there already. It could get a little crowded.'

Gently, he pushes her back down on the bed.

'I want you to close your eyes and relax.'

Obediently, Dana's eyelids droop and close. Her breathing slackens and becomes even and rhythmic.

'Now I'm going to speak to Dana,' Venkman says softly, 'and I want Dana to answer.'

Dana's lips tremble. A shadow passes across her face.

'I am Zuul. I am . . .'

'Right, you're the Gatekeeper,' Venkman says softly. 'But I want Dana. Dana, speak to me . . .'

He waits and watches, holding his breath.

Dana's eyes flick open. There is a dull red glow deep within. From her mouth issues a horrible unearthly growl, as if from some damned demonic soul:

'There is no Dana! I – am – Zuul!!'

Venkman recoils and holds out both hands placatingly.

'Whoa! Nice voice . . .'

She starts to sit up and Venkman restrains her with a light touch on the shoulder. She sinks back and closes her eyes.

'All right – Zuul. Listen carefully. I don't know where you came from or why, but I want you to get out of here and leave Dana alone. I'm going to count to ten and when I'm finished, you better be gone. Okay?'

Venkman wipes his moist palms and takes a deep breath.

'Here goes. One . . . Two . . . Three . . .'

Dana twitches. A shudder runs through her body. Her limbs start to shake. She begins to rise from the bed. Arms by her sides. Legs pressed together. Straight up into the air.

Her gown hangs beneath her in silken folds as she lies horizontally in midair, three feet above the bed.

'Wow!' Venkman gulps, both impressed and aghast. But this demonstration of unearthly power – if that's what it is – isn't over yet.

Under Venkman's astonished gaze, Dana starts to revolve until she's facing downwards, her body perfectly straight and unsupported. If this is some kind of trick, Venkman can't see how it's done.

He passes his hands underneath the full length of her body. Nothing. He kneels on the bed and ducks under to look up into her face. Her eyes slowly open and gaze down into his with a terrible burning intensity. The pupils are black and slitted.

Venkman gets out from under fast and backs across the room to the window. He stands there, rubbing his chin, contemplating the floating body and wondering what to do next.

22

'We picked up this guy and now we don't know what to do with him,' says the burly police sergeant, unlocking the rear door of the van. 'Bellevue doesn't want him and I'm afraid to put him in the lock-up. I'm telling you, there's something weird about him. And I know you guys are into this stuff, so we figured we'd check with you.'

He swings the door open for Spengler to take a look inside.

A small, thin, bedraggled figure sits forlornly on the bench. He is fastened to the wall bars with leather restraint straps, and secured to a metal ring in the floor with ankle cuffs.

Louis gazes at Spengler with a faint spark of hope, raising his sparse eyebrows.

'Are you the Gatekeeper?'

Spengler runs the PKE meter over him. The antennae spring to attention and all the lights flash like crazy.

'Bring him inside, Officer.'

Ten minutes later Louis is sitting in the basement, hooked up to a contraption of Spengler's devising. On his head he wears what looks like an aluminium

118

mixing bowl, thick skeins of multicoloured wires trailing away from dozens of electrodes.

Spengler sits hunched before a control console, monitoring the subject's etheric activity in response to questioning.

Janine leans against the workbench, gnawing her lip, unable to take her eyes off Louis. There's something about this guy that unsettles her. Something scary. But she comforts herself with the thought that Egon will know what to do. He always does.

Louis stares placidly into space, his spindly arms folded across his narrow chest. He seems perfectly content to answer Spengler's questions, speaking in a drab monotone.

In answer to a question, he intones:

'I am Vinz Clortho. Keymaster of Gozer.'

The mention of Gozer makes Spengler sit up and swing round on his stool. He leans forward, eyes blinking rapidly behind his steel-framed spectacles, and says slowly and deliberately, 'I'm Egon Spengler, Creature of Earth, Doctor of Physics, Graduate of MIT.'

Janine has picked up Louis's wallet from the workbench and is flipping through it. 'According to this, his name is Louis Tully.'

'Oh, no,' Louis contradicts her mildly. 'Tully is the fleshbag I'm using. I must wait inside for the sign.'

'Do you want some coffee while you're waiting?' Janine enquires.

Louis frowns at Spengler, as if the question is of enormous significance. 'Do I?'

'Yes, have some.'

'Yes, have some,' Louis repeats.

Janine rolls her eyes and sets a beaker of water to boil on the Bunsen burner.

'Vinz,' Spengler says with quiet urgency, watching him closely, 'what sign are you waiting for?'

Louis stares at the wall and recites blankly:

'Gozer the Traveller will come in one of the pre-chosen forms. During the rectification of the Vuldronaii the Traveller came as a very large and moving Torb. Then of course in the third reconciliation of the last of the Meketrex supplicants they chose a new form for him, that of Sloar. Many Shubs and Zuuls knew what it was to be roasted in the depths of the Sloar that day, I can tell you.'

Spengler stares at Louis for a long moment, trying to extract some sense from this, and then looks at Janine. She shakes her head and circles her temple with her finger: mad as a hatter.

The phone rings. Spengler answers it.

'Egon, it's Peter. I've got a problem.'

'What is it?'

Venkman is sitting in a chair by the bed. He glances up above his head.

'I'm with Dana Barrett and she's floating three feet off the bed.'

'Does she want to be?'

'I don't think so,' Venkman says reflectively. 'It's more of that Gozer thing. She says she's the Gatekeeper. Does that make any sense to you?'

'Some. I just met the Keymaster.' Spengler glances at the docile Louis. 'He's here with me now.'

There is a short silence, and then Venkman says, 'Do you think they ought to get together?'

'It probably wouldn't be a good idea at this point,'

which in Spengler's vocabulary amounts to a definitive veto.

'You're probably right,' Venkman agrees.

'Peter, listen to me,' Spengler says, cupping his hand round the mouthpiece and watching Louis from the corner of his eye. 'You have to keep her there. Do whatever you have to – but don't let her leave. It could be dangerous.'

'You mean . . .'

'Very dangerous,' Spengler says ominously.

'All right. I'll try.' Venkman looks nervously at the sleeping Dana for a moment. 'I'll give her 10ccs of chlorpromazine. That should keep her under. I'd better spend the night here and get back first thing in the morning.'

'All right, Peter. Good night.'

Spengler hangs up, just in time to see Louis pouring instant coffee granules into his mouth and drinking from the beaker of boiling water. He swishes the mixture round in his mouth and gulps it down with relish.

Janine sidles across to Spengler, wearing a worried frown.

She says in a low voice, 'Egon, there's something very strange about that man. I'm very psychic usually and right now I have this terrible feeling that something awful is going to happen to you.'

'Oh?'

She touches his arm and looks anxiously into his face. 'I'm afraid you're going to die.'

'Die in what sense?'

'In the physical sense.'

'I don't care,' Spengler says indifferently. 'I see us as tiny parts of a vast organism, like two bacteria

121

living on a rotting speck of dust floating in an infinite void.'

'That's so romantic,' Janine sighs, sliding her arms round him and laying her head on his chest.

Spengler stands awkwardly, not sure where to put his hands. He smiles tentatively down at her and clears his throat.

'You have nice clavicles.'

Janine blushes and hugs him to her.

Spengler swallows and looks over Janine's head to where the Keymaster sits gazing dreamily into space and humming a happy little tune while he waits for the Gatekeeper. Spengler shudders to think what might happen if they ever meet.

23

Unfortunately, that possibility is nearer than anyone realises.

And the chain of events which will precipitate it begin at ten o'clock precisely the next morning, when a cavalcade of vehicles turns into the dingy street and pulls up outside the old fire station building.

A police captain and two officers step out of the leading car and stand waiting boredly on the sidewalk for Walter Peck of the Environmental Protection Agency, Third District. With calm, imperturbable faces they watch as he climbs out of the K-car with US Government plates and tucks his briefcase under his arm.

In a moment they are joined by a technician in overalls, with a peaked cap bearing the logo of the Con Edison electric power company. He carries a large metal toolbox.

Peck glances up at the neon sign above the door, a smug and vindictive smirk on his thin lips, which doesn't go unnoticed by the captain and two officers of the New York City Police Department.

Then, with a peremptory wave of his hand, the

man from the EPA marshals his forces and leads them into the building.

'This way, Captain.'

He strides arrogantly through the garage bay en route to the basement, but is confronted at the top of the stairs by a pale and visibly-trembling Janine, beside herself with fury.

'I beg your pardon? Just where do you think you're going?'

Peck attempts to brush her aside, but Janine resists.

'Step aside, Miss, or I'll have you arrested for interfering with a police officer,' Peck says coldly, fixing her with his watery blue eyes.

'Who do you think you're talking to, Mister?' Janine blazes at him, standing her ground. 'Do I look like a child? You can't come in here without some sort of warrant or writ or something!'

Peck takes a bundle of papers from the briefcase and thrusts them under her nose. He slaps each document with the back of his hand as he rhymes off:

'Cease and desist all commerce order. Seizure of premises and chattels. Ban on the use of public utilities for non-licensed waste-handlers. And a Federal Entry and Inspection Order,' he finishes with a triumphant sneer.

Janine glowers at him, knowing she has no choice.

'This is just like Poland,' she mutters darkly as Peck brushes past her and leads the combined might of law and order and the Con Edison power company man down the stairs.

Seeing the police and government cars and the Con

Edison van parked outside the building, Venkman fears the worst.

He dashes straight in through the garage bay, hearing the voice he loves to hate as he descends to the basement. That prick Peck. The man with the buttoned-up mind.

'. . . I demand to see what's in there. Now either you shut off those "beams" or we'll shut them off for you.'

And Spengler's voice, deep and calm and polite:

'You can see what's inside through the viewing port if you wish . . .'

Venkman takes a couple of steadying breaths, and enters the basement with a nonchalant wave of his hand. He even wears a smile, at great cost to his reserves of nervous energy.

'At ease, Officers. I'm Peter Venkman. I think there's been some kind of misunderstanding here and I want to cooperate in every way I can.'

He beams round helpfully, taking in the situation at a glance.

Spengler and Janine are standing close together at the workbench, next to a little runt of a guy sitting on a stool with a vacuous look on his face. The three policemen and the Con Edison technician stand in a bemused circle, while Peck, of course, his high colour matching his beard, blue veins throbbing in his thin white neck, holds centre-stage.

The appearance of Venkman is like a red rag to a bull. Peck spins round and snarls, 'Forget it, Venkman. You had your chance to cooperate but you thought it was more fun to insult me. Now it's my turn, smart-ass.'

'He wants to shut down the laser-containment grid,' Spengler says, with a meaningful look at Venkman.

Venkman nods slowly and turns to Peck.

'If you turn that thing off, we won't be responsible for the consequences,' he says quietly.

'On the contrary! You will be held *completely* responsible!'

Peck jerks his head brusquely at the technician.

'Turn it off.'

The technician moves forward and stands in front of the control panel, scratching the back of his neck and trying to figure out what the hell the gauges, meters and winking lights are in aid of.

Venkman clenches his fist. 'Don't do it! I'm warning you!'

'I've never seen anything like this before,' the technician confesses nervously to the police captain. 'I don't know whether we . . .'

Peck hits the roof. His face goes livid. His neck throbs and his eyes bulge like wet blue pebbles.

'Just – do – it – fella!' he practically screams. 'Nobody asked you for your opinion.'

The technician looks at the captain, shrugs, and reaches up for the master control switch. Venkman leaps forward and pinions his arms. Over his shoulder, he grates at Peck through clenched teeth, 'Don't be a jerk!'

At a curt nod from the captain, the two cops bustle forward and drag Venkman off.

Peck gives Venkman a look of pure venomous hatred and says to the captain, 'If he tries that again, shoot him.'

The captain gazes at Peck with thinly-veiled contempt. 'You do your job, pencil-neck. Don't tell us how to do ours.'

'Thank you, Captain,' Venkman says, straightening his jacket as the cops release him.

Peck tightens his lips and points at the master switch. 'Now turn it off,' he orders the technician.

As the technician steps forward again, Venkman glances across at Spengler. Spengler mimes an explosion of horrendous proportions with his hands. Venkman nods and starts to back slowly towards the stairs. Spengler quietly slips his hand into Janine's and draws her with him in the same direction. Louis sees Spengler backing away and follows his example.

The technician throws the switch. The needles drop to zero. The lights flicker and die. The hum of power ceases.

Peck's expression of triumphant revenge begins to smear on his face as he feels the floor tremble under his feet. He looks wildly round, and then staggers back as the entire concrete wall of the facility starts to shudder and shake.

The mortar between the concrete blocks crumbles away, and behind them a misty pink light grows in intensity until it's blindingly bright. Suddenly one of the blocks is flung out with tremendous force, smashing into the wall opposite, and from the gap pours a thick writhing mist, shot through with glittering, dancing particles of phosphorescent light.

Running at full tilt through the garage bay, it seems to Venkman that the building itself is coming alive.

Along with the others he dashes out into the street,

the cops on their heels, an ashen-faced Peck bringing up the rear.

Venkman's feeling wasn't far wrong. From deep within the basement a column of concentrated psychokinetic energy rises up through floor after floor and erupts through the roof in a dazzling, iridescent geyser, shooting several hundred feet in the air like a stupendous Roman Candle.

Everyone ducks as a shower of ion particles, ecto-stuff and roof debris rains down. The air is acrid with choking steamy vapour.

Through it all, Louis stands and gazes upwards, the glowing geyser of energy reflected in his eyes. A rapt, beatific expression bathes his features.

'It is time. This is the sign.'

'It's a sign all right,' Janine says, shielding her head from the falling debris, choking on the foul mist.

'"Going Out Of Business".'

Louis turns sharp right and walks stiff-legged through the clamour and confusion. At the end of the street he turns sharp left and walks uptown with a steady, purposeful stride.

It is time. He must find the Gatekeeper.

24

From a point high above Manhattan you can see the glistening blue geyser erupting high into the air. Then you see it twist into a spiral of incandescent energy and turn northwards, as if drawn by a powerful magnetic field or some other natural phenomena. Conceivably – supernatural phenomena. This streamer of light, vaporous as a comet's tail, races towards the tall building to the west of Central Park. There it starts to coalesce, infusing the burnished dome with a purple glow.

Electric blue static lightning crackles over the superstructure. Over the bronze doors and marble pillars and the empty plinths. The entire peak of the building shimmers and throbs with a strange, ethereal light.

And as the bolt of energy touches the dome and travels downwards, an upper floor of the building is blasted wide open to the elements. The outer wall of an apartment completely disappears in a puff of pulverised stonework. The wide picture windows are sucked outwards into space, leaving a jagged gaping hole.

In the bedroom, Dana's eyes spring open.

Rising from the bed, she walks through the shattered apartment and stands outlined on the very edge of the gaping hole, gazing out over the city. A cool breeze ruffles her hair. Tugs at the silken shift swathing her body.

In her dark, slumberous eyes, the light of expectancy kindles and burns with feverish intensity.

It is the sign.

It is the time.

Fulfilment is at hand.

Now she must await the coming of the Keymaster.

The street is a chaos of firetrucks, police cars and public utility vehicles. The city's emergency task force, trained to deal with natural disasters and hazardous chemical spillages, has been called in.

By now the old fire station is a gutted shell surrounding the translucent blue flame, still spurting hundreds of feet into an overcast sky. Ecto-material and ionised particles shower down, coating the emergency team and the crowd of onlookers with a pinkish grey sludge.

An official from the Hazardous Chemicals Squad in a bulky protective suit and visored helmet fights his way through the mob and grabs Spengler by the arm.

'Does this stuff contain TCE, PCB or tailings from styrene esters or any polyfluoric groups?' he demands urgently.

Before Spengler can reply, the fire service chief cuts in:

'What are these pink particles? What'll happen if we use water?'

'No . . . no water.' Spengler shakes his head despairingly. 'There's nothing you can do . . .'

'What happened?'

Stantz pushes his way through the police cordon, followed by Winston. They've had to leave the Ecto-mobile half a block away. Stantz looks round at all the confusion and then up at the burning shell of the building, his bushy brows pulled together in complete and utter bewilderment.

'The storage facility blew,' Spengler explains resignedly. He nods at Peck. 'This one shut off the containment grid . . .'

Venkman is suddenly stricken with a chilling thought. He looks wildly round, squinting through the pungent vapour and showering debris.

'Where's the Keymaster?'

Spengler's long jaw drops open. 'Oh, shit!'

'Who's the Keymaster?' asks Stantz, looking blankly from one to the other.

Venkman and Spengler exchange grim glances. The ectoplasmic eruption in the basement facility is as a squib compared to what will happen if the Gatekeeper and the Keymaster ever encounter one another, and are allowed to prepare the way for Gozer.

They start off in search of Louis, but Walter Peck of the Environmental Protection Agency, Third District, is a man of stern duty and implacable responsibility.

'Stop them!' he barks at one of the police officers, and takes to jabbing his finger as he lays down the law. 'Captain, I want these men arrested. They have been acting in criminal violation of the Environmental Protection Act 1981, and this explosion was a direct result.'

Venkman gapes at him. For a second no words will come.

'*You* turned off the power!' he yells at Peck. 'You!'

He turns to the captain and tries to speak as calmly and reasonably as he can.

'Look, there was another man here. You have to find him and bring him back. He was in the basement with us . . . a short, determined-looking guy with the eyes of a happy zombie –'

'See!' Peck burbles, specks of white foam flying off his red lips, watery eyes bulging from his head. 'They are using drugs!'

Quiet, serious, studious Spengler goes for him. He gets a grip with both hands round Peck's thin neck and tries to throttle him.

'If you don't shut up I'm going to rip out your septum,' Spengler promises him faithfully.

A couple of cops haul Spengler off and support the wilting Peck, who's pulling feebly at his collar and coughing up phlegm.

The police captain has had as much as he can take. Personally, he detests this slimy little pipsqueak, and the others seem like regular guys. But in situations like this there's only one sure answer.

'I don't know what in hell's going on here, but I'm going to have to arrest you all. You can discuss it with the judge.' The captain takes out his book. 'I'm going to read you your rights now, so please listen carefully . . .'

Venkman catches Spengler's eye and shakes his head. Now the ectoplasm is really going to hit the fan.

25

Louis heads briskly uptown, watching the light show in the sky. Brilliant luminescent twisters swirling overhead. On his face, a fixed, purposeful, trance-like smile, which doesn't look at all out of place on the streets of New York. Certainly none of his fellow pedestrians streaming along Seventh Avenue notice anything out of the ordinary or pay him the slightest attention.

But if the spectacular lights in the sky are visible evidence of strange phenomena abroad in the city, stranger things still are happening on the ground.

And below ground.

A crowd of people descends the stairs into the subway on the corner of Seventh and 36th Street. As the last of them disappears into the entrance, a thin moaning whine echoes through the tiled tunnels. The crowd of people freezes, staring into the yellowish gloom. Then turns tail and flees for dear life as an impish apparition, with a shrill giggle and a flutter of its feelers, chases them back up the stairs and out into the street.

Louis walks benignly through the panic-stricken crowd as they scatter in all directions.

At the next intersection a hot-dog vendor reaches into his cart for a bun and a bag of pretzels. A look of mystification slides over his face as his hand encounters empty space. He feels around and screams. Staggers back clutching the soiled lapels of his white coat.

From out of the cart emerges the grotesque form of the Gluttonous Onion-Headed Phantasm, stuffing hot dogs, buns and pretzels into its cavernous maw. It belches loudly at the stunned customers and flits down the street, the pushcart trundling after it.

Louis walks on to Times Square.

There a nifty spirit pops out of a drain and vanishes up the exhaust pipe of a taxi. A businessman steps inside and leans back expansively, unfolding the *Wall Street Journal*.

'Gulf and Western Building! And I'm in a hurry, so let's not dawdle.'

The driver turns and touches his snap-brim cap with a skeletal claw. The decomposing face is stretched in a ghastly grin. At once the cab peels away from the kerb, executes a U-turn at fifty miles an hour in heavy traffic, and turns the wrong way up a one-way street.

With the grinning corpse at the wheel, it races at breakneck speed through the oncoming traffic, forcing cars on to the kerb and pedestrians to leap for safety. While in the back the businessman calmly puffs a large cigar and peruses the Dow Jones Index.

With a gentle, vacuous smile, Louis walks on.

In offices and shops, in bars and restaurants, in cinemas and clubs, in cabs and buses, in flophouses and the best hotels – in every highway and byway and nook and cranny throughout New York City – the ghosts come out to play.

And Louis walks on.

26

Answering that ad was the biggest mistake of his life. That's what Winston Zeddemore is telling himself now, staring through the bars of the New York City Police lock-up. Talk about *dumb*.

'We're gonna get five years for this,' he moans miserably to himself. 'Plus they're gonna make us retrap all those spooks.' He bangs his head against the bars. 'I *knew* I shouldn't have taken this job!'

In the cage behind him, Venkman, Stantz and Spengler have other thoughts to occupy them.

Spread out on a bench is a blueprint of Dana's apartment building, borrowed from the City Planning Department. Stantz has studied it in detail, and believes he's come up with the answer. Venkman feels he might be convinced as well, if only he understood half of what Stantz is jabbering on about.

Glancing over his shoulder, Venkman is uneasily aware of the other denizens of the cell, watching and listening with a mixture of intense curiosity and scowling suspicion. Not a particularly appealing bunch of individuals. Drunks, muggers, flashers, junkies and petty hoods – the bottom-of-the-barrel scrapings off the city streets.

'Look at the structure of the roof cap,' Stantz is saying, tapping the blueprint excitedly. 'It looks exactly like the kind of telemetry tracker NASA uses to identify dead pulsars in other galaxies.'

'Fabricated with magnesium-tungsten alloy,' says Spengler with a thoughtful frown. 'And look at this, Peter – cold-riveted girders with solid cores of shielded Selenium 325.'

As Venkman leans over to look, he notices they have a fascinated audience, also craning to take a peek.

'Everybody with us so far?' he asks with a bright smile.

Scratching their heads and muttering, their cellmates drift away.

'The ironwork extends down through fifty feet of bedrock and touches the water table,' Stantz goes on, looking up keenly at the others.

Venkman is impressed, but still doesn't get it. 'I guess they don't build them like they used to, huh?' he shrugs.

'No!' Stantz thumps the blueprint with his fist. 'Nobody *ever* built them like this! The architect was either an authentic whacko or a certified genius. The whole building is like one huge antenna for pulling in and concentrating psychokinetic energy.'

The light begins to dawn in Venkman's eyes at last. 'Who was the architect?'

'He's listed in the records as I. Shandor.'

'Of course!' Spengler exclaims. 'Ivor Shandor. I saw his name in Tobin's *Spirit Guide*. He started a secret society in 1920 . . .'

Venkman straightens up and folds his arms. It's all falling into place now. 'Let me guess – Gozer Worshippers.'

Spengler nods. 'Yes. After the First World War, Shandor decided that society was too sick to survive. And he wasn't alone. He had close to a thousand followers when he died. They conducted rituals – bizarre rituals – intended to bring about the end of the world.'

The more he learns about this, the less Venkman likes it. Just at the moment he can't see how Dana fits into the picture. But he has a dread feeling that when he finds out he's going to like it even less.

'She said he was "the Destructor",' he murmurs, thinking aloud.

'Who?' Spengler asks.

'Gozer.'

'You talked to Gozer?' Spengler says, confused.

'Get a grip on yourself, Egon,' Venkman tells him 'I talked to Dana Barrett and she referred to Gozer as the Destructor.'

'See?' Stantz wears a proud grin. 'I told you something big was about to happen.'

Winston stands over these three screwballs, shaking his head. He's never heard such tripe.

'This is insane! You actually believe that some mouldy Babylonian God is going to drop in at 78th and Central Park West and start tearing up the city?'

'Sumerian,' Spengler corrects him sternly. 'Not Babylonian.'

Winston snorts and banishes them to the nuthouse

with a wave of his hands and goes back to banging his head on the bars.

Dumb, dumb, *dumb*.

'Are you the Ghostbusters?'

'What about it?' Venkman asks, looking up and warily eyeing the tall, hollow-faced man in the uniform of a police inspector.

So what else can they blame them for?

'The mayor wants to see you – right away.' The police inspector nods to the guard, who unlocks the cell door.

'The whole island is going crazy.' He swings open the cell door. 'Let's go.'

27

Venkman's first impression is that City Hall is going crazy too.

Though he's relieved to find that what he took to be a lynch mob waiting on the steps is in fact a jostling, surging crowd of reporters and photographers. Questions are flung at them and a battery of cameras click as they are hustled through the pack and into the building by officials and a ten-man-strong police escort.

Inside isn't much better.

A barely-contained hysteria verging on wholesale panic seems to have infected everyone. The normal decorum of City Hall has been turned into a three-ring circus, with plenty of clowns and no ringmaster.

And at the quiet epicentre of the hurricane, four bemused and rather bewildered young men who call themselves the Ghostbusters – plucked from a prison cell and thrust into the limelight.

Venkman is used to ups and downs in his life, but all this is making even his head spin.

Led by the police inspector, the Ghostbusters are taken directly to the mayor's private office. The atmosphere is one of dignified pandemonium, with civic leaders, high-ranking officials and council aides all trying to have their say. The only problem is that none of them knows what they're talking about. New York has never had a plague of ghosts before.

The discordant babble dies away as the Ghost-busters enter. All eyes turn and regard them curiously.

The mayor shoos an aide out of his path and comes forward like a cocky prizefighter stepping to the centre of the ring. A short, thick-set man with greying hair, he has the hard, shrewd eyes of a political old pro. He's been on the ropes before and has always bounced back.

'Okay, you're the Ghostbusters,' he raps out, looking them over, weighing them up. 'And who's Peck?'

Venkman groans inside as Peck squirms forward out of the ruck, clutching a plastic folder. Already the guy is high on adrenalin, a feverish glassy glint in his watery blues.

'I'm Walter Peck, sir. And I'm prepared to make a full report.' He brandishes the dossier and points a trembling finger at the Ghostbusters. 'These men are complete snowball artists. They use nerve and sense gases to induce hallucinations. The people think they're seeing ghosts and call these bozos, who conveniently show up to get rid of the problem with a fake electronic light show –'

Stantz can't take any more of this.

'Bullshit!' He appeals to the mayor. 'Sir, this guy is responsible for the problem you're now facing. Dickless here had us turn off our laser-containment grid. That's what started it all.'

'   they probably use a mixture of gases, no doubt

141

stolen from the army,' Peck burbles on.

'Is this true?' the mayor asks, turning to Venkman.

'Yes.' Venkman nods firmly. 'This man has no dick.'

'. . . improperly stored and touched off with those high-voltage laser beams they use in their light show.' Peck is fixated with his private fantasy, a man possessed. 'That's what caused the explosion.'

The mayor looks round for help. He's out of his depth.

'All I know is,' the Fire Commissioner says quietly, 'that wasn't a light show we saw this morning. I've seen every form of combustion known to man, but this beats me.'

The Police Commissioner agrees. 'And nobody's using nerve gas on all the people that have seen those – things – all over the city.' He shakes his head soberly. 'The walls are bleeding at the 53rd Precinct. How do you explain that?'

The mayor rubs his eyes wearily and sits down behind the desk. He doesn't know who to trust or what to believe any more.

Winston feels it's his turn to say something. Pushing forward, he leans over the desk, face composed and in deadly earnest.

'I'm Winston Zeddemore, Your Honour. I've only been with the company for a couple of weeks, but I gotta tell you – these things are *real*.' He taps the desk with his knuckles. 'Since I joined these men I have seen shit that would turn you white.'

The mayor stares at Winston, goggle-eyed. He's not sure how much more of this he can stand.

There is a flurry of activity at the door, and an aide

ushers in the Archbishop of the New York Diocese, resplendent in his robes of office, complete with mitre and silver staff.

The mayor rises and rushes forward with a welcoming smile. He makes a little formal bow and kisses the Archbishop's ring. 'Your Eminence, how good of you to come. Is there anything – any advice you can possibly give us to resolve this situation?'

The Archbishop considers for a moment or two.

'Officially, the Church will not take a position on the religious implications of these . . . phenomena. However,' he goes on, with a glimmer of a mischievous smile, 'since they started, people have been lining up at every church in the city to confess and take communion. We've had to put on extra priests. Personally, I think it's a sign from God – but don't quote me on that.'

The mayor shakes his head and starts pacing. 'I can't call a press conference and tell everyone to start praying,' he says despairingly.

His haunted eye roams round the roomful of silent people and finally falls on Venkman.

'So what do I do now?'

Venkman seizes his chance.

'Mr Mayor,' he says, speaking quickly and calmly, 'it's a pretty simple choice. You can believe Mr Pecker here –'

'That's "Peck"!' snarls the bearded man from the EPA, close to breaking point.

'– or you can accept the fact that this city is heading for a disaster of really biblical proportions.'

'What do you mean, "biblical"?'

'Old Testament, Mr Mayor. Wrath-of-God type

143

stuff. The seas will boil, fire and brimstone falling from the sky . . .'

Stantz rallies round and gives it to him hard and straight.

'Forty years of darkness, earthquakes, mass hysteria, human sacrifices . . .'

'Enough!' the mayor cries. 'I get the point.' He looks distraught with indecision. 'But what if you're wrong?'

'If I'm wrong,' says Venkman with a shrug, 'then *nothing* happens, and you toss us in the can. But if I'm right, and if we can stop this thing . . . well, let's just say that you could save the lives of a lot of registered voters.'

From the expression on his face, it is clear that the mayor is giving serious consideration to this cogent and eminently rational argument. Venkman sees it, and so does Peck.

He does the bulging watery eyes bit again.

'I don't believe you're seriously considering listening to these men!'

The mayor breathes in, takes a long look at Peck, and breathes out again.

'Get him out of here,' he says shortly, and turns to Venkman, like a welterweight limbering up for the big fight.

'We've got work to do. What do you need from me?'

28

A tremor shakes the building as Louis pushes through the revolving door. The residents are evacuating. A dozen or so of them rush out of the elevator, carrying suitcases and armfuls of possessions.

Louis lets them go and then steps inside the empty elevator. His destiny is calling to him from the thirty-fifth floor.

As he comes out into the corridor, a neighbour of his, Mrs Blum, is struggling with a heavy suitcase and clutching a Siamese cat to her shapeless bosom.

'Louis! What are you doing here? Get out of the building at once! Don't you know it's an earthquake or something?'

Louis gazes right through her.

'The Traveller is coming.'

Mrs Blum purses her lips in annoyance. 'Don't be crazy. Nobody is going to come and visit you with all this commotion going on.'

She staggers past him with her burden and joins several of the other fleeing residents in the elevator. Their faces go slack with fear as yet another violent tremor rips through the structure of the building.

Louis walks past his own apartment and comes to

Dana Barrett's half-open door. He stands there for a moment and then pushes the door fully open.

A desolate wind blows through the apartment. The rubble of the shattered outer wall litters the floor. Beyond the gaping hole, Manhattan resembles a city in a tortured dream under a fitful, storm-laden sky.

And there, her slender figure in stark silhouette, stands the woman that Louis's unconscious mind has been lusting after for 8,000 years.

He moves towards her and they meet face to face on the brink of the crumbling precipice. A tremor shakes the building and Louis's innermost being. His voice squeaks with tremulous excitement.

'Are you the Gatekeeper?'

Dana stands magnificently before him, her eyes probing down into his, her lips parted in voluptuous invitation.

She smiles. She speaks.

'I am Zuul.'

She reaches forward and takes the ecstatic Louis in her arms and bends over his tiny swooning form in a crushing embrace.

Louis submits. He clings and sinks beneath her on to the couch.

A shaft of lightning cleaves the storm-tumbled sky.

Thunder rumbles across the dark heavens.

The building shudders with its passing.

The earth moves.

Stantz is loading their gear into the Ectomobile while Spengler and Winston are charging the proton packs from the City Hall power supply. Venkman stands on the loading dock, conferring with a police captain and two officers.

The captain reports briskly that preparations are already under way.

'We've cleared the whole apartment building on Central Park West and cordonned off 78th Street. I'm massing our own special tactics squad and the National Guard is on stand-by.'

'Better alert the Red Cross too,' Venkman suggests.

The rear of City Hall is a hive of activity. True to his word, the mayor has placed every resource and facility at their disposal. Now it's up to them.

Venkman jumps down and joins the others. They don their jumpsuits and run a final check on the equipment. The proton packs are charged, the particle throwers primed. Between them they have enough ecto-traps to ensnare a regiment of ghosts and ghouls, spirits and spooks.

Venkman gathers them round for a last word.

'Okay. Just remember – whatever happens out there, we are total professionals. Not only are we the best Ghostbusters around, we're the *only* Ghostbusters around. It's all up to us.'

'Let's roll!'

At Venkman's shout and signal, the motorcade moves off through the gates of City Hall. With a vanguard of police outriders and two armoured police cruisers bringing up the rear, the silvery Ectomobile speeds uptown, strobes flashing, siren wailing.

Cars pull over to let them pass. People on the

sidewalks stand and gawp. Midtown Manhattan practically comes to a stop.

Soon they're past Columbus Circle and heading up
Central Park West.

This is it.

Here they come . . .

Here come the Ghostbusters!

29

The Ectomobile pulls up outside the building, the doors fly open and the Ghostbusters leap out.

Immediately, a roar erupts from the hundreds of people lining the street, held back by the police barriers. Every class, creed and colour is there, cheering themselves hoarse as Venkman, ever the showman, clasps both hands above his head in the gesture of a contender going into battle for the big one.

'Get 'em, Ghostbusters!' screams a groupie girl, eyes wild with excitement.

'All *right*, Ghostbusters!' yells a punk with shaved head and daubed face. 'Go get 'em!'

And the cry echoes down the street, from a crowd whipped up to fever-pitch:

'Ghostbusters! Ghostbusters! Ghostbusters! Ghostbusters!'

Stantz hauls out the formidable weaponry from the back of the Ectomobile and the four men kit themselves up, buckling on their proton packs, checking power levels, hefting their lethal quantum energy throwers.

Together they form a tight circle and shake hands.

Keyed-up and ready to go, Venkman looks at each man in turn.

'Are we all together on this now?'

Answering nods. They all are. Winston has a fleeting afterthought, which he feels he ought to voice at this point.

'Only that I think we should get on a plane right now and go to Australia or Indonesia until this blows over.'

Venkman nods. He considers that this brainwave has a lot to recommend it. 'I'm going to make a note of your suggestion and possibly bring it up later if this thing really gets out of hand. Now let's move!'

As they turn and head for the entrance, a flash of lightning from the temple rooftop casts a brilliant, blinding light over the street. The building appears to tilt crazily. The sidewalk under their feet shifts and rears up, as if under enormous pressure. A crack zigzags the length of the pavement and the four Ghostbusters lose their balance and topple into the yawning crevasse.

A tense hush settles over the crowd. The dust slowly settles and clears. Then a grimy hand claws its way out of the chewed-up concrete rubble and Stantz's beaming face pops up. A relieved cheer rings out, and then another, as the Ghostbusters, alive and well, clamber out of the pit.

Raising their left fists in gestures of defiance, they enter the building, the cheers and applause of the crowd ringing in their ears.

Thirty-five flights of stairs later, their defiance seems to have deserted them.

Gasping and coughing, they stagger from the stairwell into the corridor, and sag weakly against the walls.

'I'm glad we took the stairs,' Venkman remarks, heaving for breath. Nobody laughs.

Outside Dana's apartment they halt and stand in a shuffling group, looking uneasily at the charred and blackened door-frame.

Venkman calls Dana's name, softly at first, and then louder.

The only sound is a thin moaning wind.

'Maybe we should go downstairs and call first?' Winston suggests politely.

Venkman waves him to silence and gently pushes the door. It falls off its hinges and crashes to the floor, revealing the scene of devastation within.

Cautiously, with mounting trepidation, the Ghostbusters enter the wrecked apartment. Shredded curtains flutter in the stiff breeze blowing clean across the city and through the space where once there was a wall. The furniture has been swept into a jumbled, splintered heap in one corner.

'Well, she's not here,' Winston says cheerfully, halfway to the door. 'Let's go.'

The others turn to follow, when Stantz spots something. An interior wall has been blasted away, and through the hole of crumbling plaster and brick can be seen a winding stone stairway.

Stantz steps over the rubble towards it.

'Hey, where do these stairs lead?'

'Up,' Venkman says, and slaps him on the shoulder. 'Go!'

Stantz scowls. The same old Venkman. Always last to go first.

He squares his jaw and leads the assault up the stairway. Close on his heels, the others charge up the stone steps, all four Ghostbusters emerging on to the roof in time to witness the most incredible sight of their lives.

The transformation of flesh-and-blood humans into mythical beasts.

Outlined against the bruised and angry sky, Dana and Louis stand on the empty stone plinths, facing the dome of the temple. Fierce blue sparks of pure energy crackle over the stonework of the building. From above – from a point higher than the dome itself – two beams lance down and transfix them within an aura of glowing plasma. They bend. They crouch. They grow a thick leathery hide. Their skulls broaden and flatten and sprout horns. Their hands elongate into splayed paws with curved black talons.

No longer Dana and Louis on the plinths, but two massive snarling Terror Dogs, with slitted black pupils in their glowing orbs of eyes.

Venkman looks at the others. The others look at Venkman.

'All right,' he concedes. 'She's a dog.'

But now a transformation is happening to the temple. With a ponderous groaning and grating of stone, the walls begin to separate and to open, revealing its secret architecture. A broad marble staircase stretches into the hazy distance, and beyond, a huge translucent pyramid hangs suspended in the air.

A bright white light starts to descend the staircase.

As it floats nearer, the glowing sphere of light slowly changes and solidifies into a form that is vaguely human.

Or perhaps superhuman.

The form of an immensely tall, slender and beautiful woman clad in dazzling silver.

Raising her hand, she beckons the Terror Dogs to her. They leap from their plinths and stand fawning as she strokes and fondles them.

'I thought Gozer was a man?' Stantz whispers, awestruck by the beauty and terror of this shimmering silver vision.

Spengler puts him right. 'It can take any form it desires.'

As if becoming aware of their presence for the first time, the woman turns her gaze upon them. The Ghostbusters quake in their boots. Her eyes are pits of hellish flame.

'Are you sure it's Gozer?' Venkman asks, gulping. He doesn't want to pick an argument with the wrong person.

'Only one way to find out,' Stantz says. Taking a brave step forward, he sticks his chest out and calls out sharply, 'Gozer the Gozerian?'

The other three cower behind Stantz, wondering if he's taken leave of his senses. Apparently he has, for Stantz goes on sternly, like a traffic cop handing out a ticket:

'As a duly-constituted representative of the City of New York, and on behalf of the County and State of New York, the United States of America, the Planet Earth and all its inhabitants, I hereby order you to cease and desist any and all supernatural activity and return at once to your place of origin or next parallel dimension.'

'Well, that ought to do it,' Venkman murmurs drily in Stantz's ear.

Gozer draws herself up to her full imposing height and asks curiously, 'Are you a god?'

Stantz shrugs. 'No.'

Gozer raises both arms high –

'Then die!'

– and sends searing bolts of energy from her fingertips which blast the Ghostbusters and send them tumbling to the very edge of the roof.

Shaking his dazed head, Winston says furiously, 'You should've said "yes"! She might have been willing to negotiate.'

Venkman untangles himself and gets up. He is mad now. Spitting mad. He unclips his thrower and sets the control.

'Okay. That's it! I'm gonna turn this Gozer into toast.'

In line abreast, the Ghostbusters mount the marble stairs, activating their proton drivers for an entrapment. The fun and games are over. Now they mean business.

Taking careful aim, Venkman looses off a curling stream of particles. Gozer stands with legs apart, as if bracing herself to take the full quantum shock – and then leaves the ground in a leap of superhuman agility. Soaring high above their heads, she does a perfect double-flip in midair and lands behind them on the stone balustrade encircling the roof.

The Ghostbusters spin round, jaws dropping open with incredulous amazement.

'Nimble little minx, isn't she?' Venkman mutters.

'Forget the trapping!' Stantz urges, his dander up. 'Just blast her!'

The Ghostbusters adjust their throwers to maximum charge.

Bunched together in a tight group, they unleash four streams at peak concentration which converge on the target in a deadly blaze of destructive power.

It seems at first that Gozer can withstand even this. Her body absorbs the blast without strain, her face a smooth calm mask.

Then in a vivid pink flash of light, she vanishes.

Leaving behind a husk of carbonised particles which are quickly borne away on the wind.

In the long silence that follows, Venkman looks at the others, stunned. Is that it? Have they won? Even the Terror Dogs, with the annihilation of their god, have petrified into stone.

Winston is in no doubt. He lets out a whoop of triumph.

'We did it! We did it! Thank God!'

Stantz bounds down the staircase, beaming broadly. 'We neutronised her! She's a molecular nonentity!'

Venkman wipes the sweat from his brow. He's beginning to believe it himself now, and looks at Spengler with a relieved smile.

But Spengler is busy scanning the temple with his PKE meter. Spengler studies the reading and frowns. Spengler isn't so sure.

30

Somebody or something is moving the building on its foundations. The Ghostbusters look at each other in alarm as the entire edifice shudders and sways. Cracks appear in the ornate stone mouldings. Carvings break away and topple into the street far below.

From out of the dark clouds, a single bolt of lightning strikes the temple dome. A thunderclap reverberates from on high and rocks the rooftop.

Venkman has the uncomfortable feeling that they've made somebody mad.

The Ghostbusters raise their eyes fearfully as a voice speaks to them from the heavens. The being in human female form wasn't apparently the genuine Gozer, merely some kind of surrogate. But there can be no question now, not the slightest shadow of doubt.

This is The Real Thing.

'SUBCREATURES!' the voice thunders, loud enough to be heard throughout Metropolitan New York and parts of New Jersey.

'GOZER THE GOZERIAN, GOZER THE DESTRUCTOR, VOL-GUUS ZILDROHAR, THE TRAVELLER HAS COME. CHOOSE AND PERISH!'

Venkman looks over his shoulder. 'Is he talking to us?'

'What's he talking about?' Winston asks blankly. 'Choose what?'

Stantz cups his hands and shouts up into the stormy sky.

'What do you mean, "choose"? We don't understand.'

'CHOOSE!!!'

The word rocks the Ghostbusters back on their heels.

Spengler says thoughtfully, 'I think he's saying that since we're about to be sacrificed anyway, we get to choose the form we want it to take.'

Stantz stares at him. 'You mean if I stand here and concentrate on the image of J. Edgar Hoover, Gozer will appear as J. Edgar Hoover and wipe us out?'

'That appears to be the case,' Spengler replies gravely.

The awful possibility dawns on Venkman. He swings round and faces the others.

'Don't think of anything! Clear your minds. We only get one crack at this –'

'THE CHOICE IS MADE. THE TRAVELLER HAS COME!'

'No!' Venkman shouts, panic rising in his throat. '– We didn't choose anything!'

He looks wildly at Spengler. 'I didn't think of an image, did you?'

'No.'

They both look at Winston.

'My mind's a total void!'

All three look at Stantz.

He lowers his eyes sheepishly. 'I couldn't help it.'

He gulps and confesses guiltily, 'It just popped in there.'

'*What* popped in there?' asks Venkman dangerously.

'Look!'

Everyone turns to where Winston is pointing. Something big and white and blobby is moving in the area of Columbus Circle. And it is *huge* – dwarfing the buildings around it. Distantly, they can hear the sound of giant footsteps, like seismic shock waves, plodding nearer and nearer.

'What is it, Ray?' Venkman asks, his voice thin with desperation. 'What did you think of?'

Through the buildings they glimpse what appears to be a fat white arm, the size of a hot-air balloon.

Stantz is in shock. He sags weakly at the knees. He keeps repeating, 'It can't be . . . it can't be . . . it can't be . . .' in faint gasps of disbelief.

The huge white blob plods onward up Central Park West. Its chest, the size of a football field, comes into view, and then its massive smiling face, broad as a billboard.

The Ghostbusters gape in utter stupefaction. It can't be, but it is. All ten storeys tall of it.

'It's . . .' Stantz squeaks. 'It's . . . Mr. the Stay-Puft Marshmallow Man!'

The cute, loveable figure, the brand symbol on ten billion packs of chewy marshmallow, adored by generations of American kids, is coming to get them .   arms and legs made of soft, puffy blocks, body smooth and white and round, topped by a bobbing, laughing head of square marshmallow.

Cute and warm and loveable all right, if only he wasn't the size of Godzilla.

Stantz has collapsed over the stone plinth. He bleats pitifully, 'I tried to think of the most harmless thing . . . something that could never destroy us . . . something I loved from my childhood . . .'

'And you came up with *that*?' Venkman says, goggling at him.

'The Mr. Stay-Puft Marshmallow Man!' Winston says, slack-jawed.

'He was on all the packages we used to buy when I was a kid,' says Stantz, fondly remembering. 'We used to roast Stay-Puft marshmallows at Camp Waconda . . .'

'Great!' says Venkman grimly. 'The marshmallows are about to get their revenge.'

His big soft white feet stepping on cars and lampposts and mailboxes and squashing them flat, the marshmallow man plods merrily towards them, head bobbing jauntily up and down with each twelve-foot stride.

He arrives at 78th Street and turns his laughing face up to look at the building. Then, in a single stride, crosses the street and plants his foot on to the roof of the church next door, using it as a stepping-stone to climb the building.

Peering over the edge, the Ghostbusters watch in silence as the Mr. Stay-Puft Man clambers towards them.

'What now?' Venkman asks, dry-mouthed.

'Full-stream with strogon pulse,' Spengler says decisively, unclipping his thrower and setting the control.

159

Venkman and Stantz look at each other. They both shrug.

'I guess that's all we've got,' Venkman says quietly.

The Ghostbusters line up on the edge of the roof, weapons drawn, steeling themselves to face the Attack of the Hundred-Foot Mr. Stay-Puft Marshmallow Man.

31

The crowd in the street below has scattered, fleeing the marshmallow man's ponderous tread, leaving behind the two police cruisers with half-a-dozen cops sheltering behind them.

Crouching there, powerless to do anything, they stare upwards with their hearts in their mouths as the Mr. Stay-Puft Man climbs the sheer face of the building, clinging with marshmallow fingertips to windowsills and sliding marshmallow toes along ledges.

A man with a red beard, watery blue eyes and a thin neck runs up the street and grabs the police captain by the shoulder.

'Are the Ghostbusters up there?' demands Walter Peck, white to the lips with rage.

'Yeah.'

'I want you to go up on the roof and arrest them,' Peck says in total seriousness. 'This time they've gone too far.'

The captain looks at Peck as if he's insane and knocks his hand away.

'You arrest them, numb nuts!'

Peck strides to the middle of the street and stands there, hands on hips, fuming and impotent.

High above, the Ghostbusters brace themselves as the marshmallow monster climbs within range. As his huge laughing face swells beneath them, Venkman shouts the order:

'Hit him!'

Four curling streams spit out and engulf the Mr. Stay-Puft Man in a crossfire of searing energy. Scorching holes ringed with blue flame appear in his chest and belly and spread along his arms and legs. Bellowing with pain and rage, the monster flails his huge arms as flaming hunks of melting marshmallow start to peel off, revealing an empty skeletal rib-cage.

'Good,' Winston says with a lame grin. 'Now we made him mad.'

Massive sticky globs of toasted marshmallow splatter the street below, like giant cowpats.

Peck panics and decides this isn't the best place to be. He turns left. He turns right. He looks up.

Too late.

A hunk as big as a bus scores a direct hit, burying him up to the neck in half-a-ton of hot sticky sucrose.

Venkman is becoming philosophical in his old age. 'We're going to be killed by a hundred-foot marshmallow,' he remarks calmly to no one in particular.

It certainly looks that way as the Mr. Stay-Puft Man still comes on, most of his chest melted away, his laughing head a fireball of blue flame. Looming over them, he raises a burning fist, about to swipe them into eternity.

Is this it? Are the Ghostbusters about to meet a sticky end?

'One . . . two . . . three . . .' Venkman counts, readying them for the final onslaught. Everyone raises their weapons – everyone except Spengler, who has just come up with the best idea of his life.

'No! Them! Shoot them!'

He points at the Terror Dogs, frozen into studies of petrified motion on the marble steps.

'Cross the beams!' Spengler yells.

Venkman swings round and then hesitates.

'But you said crossing the beams would be bad! It'll kill her! And us!'

'Life is just a state of mind,' Spengler tells him.

'But it's my favourite state.'

'Either way we're history,' says Stantz, grim-faced.

They fire.

If Venkman expects it to be horrendous, he is disappointed. It is even worse.

At the focal point of the crossed beams, an intense white-hot globe of plasma explodes like a miniature hydrogen bomb, obliterating the Terror Dogs and the temple in a shock wave of heat and light.

Blown off their feet by the blast, the Ghostbusters watch with dazed eyes and numbed senses as the marshmallow monster is whirled about in a spinning tornado and tossed up high in a cyclonic firestorm.

Then, from deep inside, an explosion rips apart the whirling, flaming carcase. Molten marshmallow sprays out and spatters down, drenching the rooftop in a thick white viscous layer.

Above the skyscrapers of Manhattan, the dark clouds are suddenly caught up in a powerful whirlpool of wind. Swirling faster and faster, it sucks the flaming mass of gas and carbonised ash straight up into the centre of the vortex.

The dark clouds are sucked with it, diminishing into a hazy brown speck, which seconds later vanishes into the stratosphere.

As if swept clean by a gigantic vacuum cleaner, a beautiful clear blue sky stretches as far as the eye can see.

Covered in clinging gunge, the Ghostbusters crawl out from the shelter of the parapet and look about them.

The once magnificent temple is now in ruins. The Terror Dogs, barely recognisable under a crust of blackened carbon, are fused to their pedestals.

This time there can be no doubt. With the destruction of his earthly portal, the god Gozer has been banished for ever to a distant dimension.

Venkman mounts the cracked marble staircase and gazes with a heavy heart at the charred remains of the Terror Dogs. He feels no sense of victory or triumph. The Ghostbusters might have won.

But Venkman has lost.

32

A scratching sound makes him lean closer. A slight movement in one of the paws catches his eye.

Hardly daring to believe or to hope, Venkman watches a chunk of the charred crust fall away.

Inside there is a hand. A human hand. A human female hand.

Venkman tears into the black coating, ripping it apart. An arm appears, and then Dana's face, bemused, begrimed, blinking in the bright sunshine.

Venkman pulls her clear and helps her to stand.

'Are you all right?'

'Oh, sure.' Dana leans against him, swept by a wave of dizziness. 'I'm getting used to this.'

Stantz and Spengler free Louis, who staggers to his feet. Seeing Dana, a spasm of guilty panic crosses his face.

'I'm innocent! Honest, Dana, I never touched you. Not that I remember, anyway.'

Coming to her senses, Dana glares round at everyone. 'All right, what happened to me?'

'Nothing!' says Venkman, poker-faced 'We just got rid of that thing in your kitchen.'

'Really! Is it gone?'

'Yeah – along with most of your furniture and a lot of your personal possessions. This one took some work.'

'Thank you,' says Dana ruefully. 'Next time I want to break a lease I'll know who to call.'

Venkman slips his arm around her waist and looks into her eyes. 'This is going to cost you, you know. Our fees are ridiculously high.'

Dana kisses him on the cheek, then nods at Louis. 'Talk to my accountant.'

Louis takes in the wrecked temple and rubs his hands. 'Oh, great! I bet we could write off all the damage as an Act of God.'

Led by Venkman and Dana, arm in arm, the Ghostbusters emerge from the building to a deafening ovation. From end to end, the entire length of 78th Street is jammed with happy, jubilant New Yorkers.

Janine rushes up and hugs Spengler, whose long face breaks into a shy smile.

Standing in front of the Ectomobile, the best – and only – Ghostbusters wave to the crowd, acknowledging the cheers and applause. Kids astride their parents' shoulders, wearing Ghostbusters T-shirts, wave back excitedly.

Dana laughs as Venkman leaps to the barrier and starts shaking hands and kissing babies, as if he were running for president. And even when they're all in the Ectomobile and driving down Central Park West, lights flashing, siren wailing, he's giving the wildly cheering crowd all he's got.

But Venkman's no fool. This is a goodwill investment in the future of Ghostbusters Inc.

Maybe tomorrow, maybe next week – but some time soon – a lot of these people are going to be awakened by ghosts and ghouls and things that go bump in the night.

And when that happens, they'll know who to call. Right?

GHOSTBUSTERS

THE MAKING OF
THE FILM

New York City has a problem: paranormal occur-
rences have been plaguing the city in increasing numbers and the only ones who know this are three
extraordinarily bright, slightly offbeat university
parapsychologists who lose their research grant, are
forced out of academia and start their own business
– 'Ghostbusters.'

Bill Murray, Dan Aykroyd, Sigourney Weaver,
Harold Ramis and Rick Moranis star in Columbia
Pictures' new comedy, 'Ghostbusters,' produced and
directed by Ivan Reitman, co-written by Aykroyd
and Ramis.

In a virtual coup, combining the consummate comic
talents of our time in one film, 'Ghostbusters' pairs
Bill Murray and Dan Aykroyd together on screen for
the first time, and reunites Ivan Reitman and Harold
Ramis ('Animal House,' 'Meatballs' and 'Stripes').

The unique talents of Murray, Aykroyd, Ramis
and Reitman are brought together to create a contemporary, new-generation comedy. In 'Ghostbusters,'
Murray, Aykroyd and Ramis portray cosmic cru-
saders who, because of their advanced intelligence,

walk that fine line between genius and lunacy – that they are parapsychologists adds yet another ingredient to this fine comic stew.

'The "Ghostbusters" and I go way back,' says director Reitman. 'I first worked with Dan when I was directing television in Toronto. The show was called "Greed," and Dan was the announcer. The show had so little money that Dan had to kick back half of his salary to us each week. I started working with Bill and Harold on a stage revue I directed in New York called "The National Lampoon Show," which also starred Gilda Radner and John Belushi. Since then, of course, I've worked with Bill and Harold on a number of features and am pleased to finally be working with Dan again.'

'The opportunity to do a comedy with Bill, Dan, Harold and Rick Moranis, who plays my weird neighbour, was part of the great appeal the film had for me,' adds co-star Sigourney Weaver. Her character, Dana, calls the Ghostbusters for help. 'I knew the work would be loose, crazy and spontaneous. I've worked on the stage, so I've done a lot of improvisation, but this was a different atmosphere for film. Having come out of Second City, the guys were all very generous. There was no ego on this show. It was all very giving, which was wonderful.'

'We approached "Ghostbusters" from the point of view of a team,' says co-writer/co-star Harold Ramis. 'My character, Spengler, is the brains because I tend to be rationalistic. Danny's character, Stantz, is the heart because he tends to be enthusiastic and sincere, and Bill's character, Venkman, is the mouth because he really can talk. Together, we add up to a whole person.'

'Ghostbusters' is the brainchild of Dan Aykroyd. After writing the first draft of the script himself, Aykroyd brought in Ramis, Reitman and Murray. A card-carrying member of the American Society for Psychical Research, Aykroyd believes that ghosts and American humour are linked in film history by groups like Laurel and Hardy, Abbott and Costello, the Bowery Boys, Dean Martin and Jerry Lewis, and Bob Hope. 'All comedy performers have dealt with ghosts in some of their work,' says Aykroyd. 'We're just doing the modern version of the old-time ghost movies. The only difference is that we have a little more theory, perhaps a little more science and a lot more technology than our predecessors.'

In June of 1983, Ivan Reitman began assembling his production team. Production designer John De Cuir and visual effects supervisor Richard Edlund were brought in not only because of their impeccable credentials but because of their unique experience with large-scale productions. De Cuir has won Academy Awards for 'The King and I,' 'Cleopatra' and 'Hello, Dolly!', Edlund for 'Star Wars,' 'The Empire Strikes Back,' 'Raiders of the Lost Ark' and 'Return of the Jedi.' The well-respected cinematographer Laszlo Kovacs joined the group, as did the talented and prolific costume designer Theoni V. Aldredge. Michael Gross and Joe Medjuck came on board as associate producers.

'Ghostbusters' presented its filmmakers with some unusual design problems – from a rooftop temple to the exotic equipment the Ghostbusters would carry. 'Part of the package that Dan delivered to me with that first draft was a series of illustrations that showed some of the equipment he felt the Ghostbusters would use to apprehend the various ghosts, what some of the ghouls would look like and what their vehicle would look like,' says Reitman.

Production began in October of 1983 in New York City. For its month-long stay, 'Ghostbusters' used locations that included the New York Public Library, City Hall, Columbia University, Tavern on the Green, Central Park West, Columbus Circle and the old New York Police Department lock-up, among others.

Shooting on Central Park West, the location for Dana and Louis' ghost-infested apartment building, was not only a complicated proposition for the film-makers but for the city of New York as well. 'At times we had four or five hundred extras working,' says associate producer Joe Medjuck. 'As if blocking the traffic on Central Park West wasn't bad enough, we also ended up blocking the crosstown traffic coming through Central Park. At one time, I think we had the whole upper-third of Manhattan in gridlock. The police department and the film commission gave us all the necessary permits, but they also put restrictions on us – the biggest of which was that we could only work until midnight. However, because we were under the gun, a kind of excitement grew, and I think you can see it in the footage we have of those huge crowd scenes.'

'Ivan had good preparation for those scenes – particularly for the physical side of it,' adds Ramis.

172

'When we were doing "Stripes" you could see how Ivan loved to call out the tanks when we were shooting at Fort Knox. He had 700 soldiers, as many tanks as he needed, heavy artillery, mortars. He was like a kid in a toy store.'

Meanwhile, back in Los Angeles, John De Cuir's crew was nearing completion of the temple set at The Burbank Studios. Standing over sixty feet tall, the set covered an entire sound stage and cost over $1 million to build. It was surrounded by a backlit, 360-degree panorama of New York City. 'The top of the Central Park West building is probably one of the most complicated sets we've ever built,' comments production designer John De Cuir. 'We've had some like "Cleopatra" where we built cities and barges all over the world, and we've had 'The Agony and the Ecstasy' where we had to construct the Sistine Chapel. But with this one, Ivan's played it against the great tapestry of New York – the real New York – so, of course, we had to live up to it in Hollywood on the studio sets.'

'Despite blowing up streets and having close to 500 extras, cast and crew members running around, we got out of New York two and a half days ahead of schedule,' remembers associate producer Michael Gross. 'Then we went right on to Stage 16 in Burbank, where the big set was, and it immediately ground us to a halt. We figured it would be simple to shoot because we were on the safety of a set, but the set was so big! It required so much light that Laszlo Kovacs had to use fourteen of the existing sixteen largest spotlights ever built in Hollywood. The whole studio has the capacity to supply 80,000 amps, and we needed 50,000. They actually had to shut down other stages when we shot. Stage 16 was surrounded by huge generators, we had twelve separate vehicles generating power whenever we turned on the lights.'

The interior of Dana's apartment and a partial hotel set were built on a second sound stage. Additional Los Angeles shooting was done at a downtown fire station, MacArthur Park, the Biltmore Hotel and The Burbank Studios' ranch, where a two-storey façade of Dana's Central Park West apartment building was re-created.

All the while, Richard Edlund and his staff at Entertainment Effects Group (in conjunction with Boss Film Corporation) had been creating the 200 special effects shots required for 'Ghostbusters.' Working at their shop in Marina del Rey and on the sound stages at The Burbank Studios, they created creatures and ghosts with stop-motion, rotoscoping and cell animation. Using miniatures, they re-created the Central Park West apartment building and brought to life the various fates that befall it.

After fifteen weeks of shooting, 'Ghostbusters' finally wrapped in February.

The music for 'Ghostbusters' is being supplied by some of the hottest acts in music today. In addition to the score by Elmer Bernstein and the title song by Ray Parker Jr., there is original music from Laura Branigan, the Thompson Twins, Air Supply, the Alessi Brothers, the Bus Boys and Mick Smiley. There is also a music video, directed by Ivan Reitman and featuring Bill Murray and Dan Aykroyd, with Ray Parker Jr. performing the 'Ghostbusters' title song. The soundtrack album is available on Arista Records.

About the Cast . . .

BILL MURRAY stars as Venkman in 'Ghost-busters,' which marks his third outing with director Ivan Reitman (after the successful 'Meatballs' and 'Stripes'). Back in an all-out comedy after his por-trayal of Larry Darrell in the soon-to-be-released 'The Razor's Edge,' Murray is right at home with his co-stars and director, alumni of 'Saturday Night Live,' 'The National Lampoon Show' and/or SCTV in varied combinations.

Murray was born in Evanston, Illinois, and raised in nearby Wilmette. He won a scholarship to Chicago's Second City Workshop and later went to New York, where he joined 'The National Lampoon Radio Show.' In 1975 he joined the off-Broadway satirical revue 'The National Lampoon Show,' along with John Belushi, Harold Ramis, Gilda Radner and brother Brian Doyle-Murray. Following a stint on 'Saturday Night Live With Howard Cosell,' Lorne Michaels chose him for his 'NBC's Saturday Night Live.'

After four years as one of the 'Not Ready for Prime Time Players' with, among others, John Belushi and Dan Aykroyd, Murray took his first feature role as Tripper in 'Meatballs,' which was directed by Ivan Reitman and co-written by Harold Ramis.

Murray's re-teaming with Reitman and Ramis in Columbia's 'Stripes' was enormously successful and firmly established Murray as one of America's finest comic actors. More recently, he starred as Dustin Hoffman's roommate in 'Tootsie' and as Larry Dar-rell in 'The Razor's Edge,' a film which he co-wrote with its director John Byrum.

DAN AYKROYD, one of the original stars of 'NBC's Saturday Night Live,' continues his string of motion-picture comedy roles as Stantz in 'Ghostbusters.'

In one of the smash-hit films of 1983, Aykroyd starred with yet another 'SNL' player, Eddie Murphy, in 'Trading Places,' in which he played an arrogant, wealthy snob stripped of his riches.

Born and raised in Canada, Aykroyd was a rather rebellious youth who dropped out of school and joined the Toronto company of the Second City improvisational troupe, where he developed his comic talents. While a member of Second City, Aykroyd was spotted by 'Saturday Night Live' executive producer Lorne Michaels and cast as an actor and writer for five seasons of 'SNL.' Aykroyd's uncanny impressions of Tom Snyder, Richard Nixon and Jimmy Carter, as well as scores of original creations, including the Coneheads and the Blues Brothers (with John Belushi), propelled him to stardom.

After winning an Emmy Award in 1977 for his work on 'Saturday Night Live,' Aykroyd made his film debut in 1979 with Steven Spielberg's '1941'. His next film was John Landis's international success 'The Blues Brothers' with John Belushi, which was followed in 1982 with another Belushi collaboration, John Avildsen's 'Neighbors.'

More recently, Aykroyd starred in 'Dr. Detroit,' appeared in 'Twilight Zone – The Movie' and starred with Eddie Murphy in 'Trading Places.' Together with Harold Ramis, Aykroyd co-wrote the screenplay for 'Ghostbusters.'

SIGOURNEY WEAVER is Dana in 'Ghostbusters.'
Born in New York City to former NBC president
Sylvester 'Pat' Weaver and English actress Elizabeth
Inglis, Miss Weaver changed her first name from
Susan to Sigourney, a minor character in F. Scott
Fitzgerald's 'The Great Gatsby.' She attended the
Brearley, Chaplin and Ethel Walker schools before
going to Stanford University, where she studied Eng-
lish literature. Upon graduation, she enrolled in the
Yale University School of Drama, from which she
received an M.F.A. Her first professional job was as
understudy in Sir John Gielgud's production of 'The
Constant Wife' starring Ingrid Bergman. She sub-
sequently appeared in several productions for Joseph
Papp in New York, as well as in the off-Broadway
productions 'Gemini,' 'Marco Polo Sings a Solo' and
'New Jerusalem.'

Following roles on television in 'The Best of Fami-
lies' and the daytime drama 'Somerset,' Miss Weaver
broke into films with Ridley Scott's 'Alien'. Next came
the part of the newscaster in 'Eyewitness' for director
Peter Yates opposite William Hurt, after which Aus-
tralian director Peter Weir tapped her for the lead
opposite Mel Gibson in 'The Year of Living Dangerously.' Miss Weaver next starred with Chevy Chase
and Gregory Hines in 'Deal of the Century.' Most
recently, she co-starred with Harvey Keitel, William
Hurt and Christopher Walken in 'Hurly Burly,' a
play directed by Mike Nichols at the Goodman
Theatre in Chicago.

For HAROLD RAMIS, who stars as Spengler in
'Ghostbusters,' the film reunites him with old friends

and colleagues. Having previously teamed with Bill Murray and Ivan Reitman on screen with 'Meatballs' and 'Stripes,' and performed with 'Saturday Night Live' players such as Bill Murray, John Belushi and Gilda Radner during his National Lampoon days, this is his first time in tandem with Dan Aykroyd, which, in a way, completes the overall picture.

In his most recent directorial outing, Ramis presided over a cast that included Chevy Chase in 'National Lampoon's Vacation,' one of 1983's summer hits.

Although Ramis is better known as a writer and director (having co-written 'Animal House,' 'Meatballs' and 'Caddyshack' and having directed 'Caddyshack' and 'National Lampoon's Vacation'), he has solid acting credentials. His first film role was opposite Bill Murray in 'Stripes,' though he performed with the Second City TV troupe and also toured with the Second City Road Company from 1976 to 1978. In 1975 he appeared in the satirical revue, 'The National Lampoon Show,' produced by Ivan Reitman, in which Ramis was a featured player with newcomers Bill Murray, John Belushi, Brian Doyle-Murray and Gilda Radner.

'Ghostbusters,' which Ramis co-wrote and in which he stars, marks his fourth film association with both Bill Murray and Ivan Reitman.

Emmy Award-winner RICK MORANIS is Louis in 'Ghostbusters.' In less than two years Moranis, who joined 'SCTV' in 1980, created with fellow SCTV-er Dave Thomas the now-famous Canadian 'hosers,' the McKenzie Brothers, cut an album which went gold, and wrote, directed and starred in the film 'Strange Brew.'

While in high school in his native Toronto, Moranis began working part time at a radio station, which led to a job with the Canadian Broadcasting Corporation (CBC) in which he engineered and produced radio shows, as well as writing material for the disc jockeys. He began writing and acting for CBC on radio and television, wrote and performed in two pilots for CBC, and appeared nationally on CBC on 'The Alan Hamel Show' and '90 Minutes Live.'

Moranis joined Second City Television Company in 1980, during which time he co-created the McKenzie Brothers and earned acclaim for his portrayals of such personalities as Woody Allen, Dick Cavett and Merv Griffin. 'SCTV' went network on NBC in 1981 and Moranis earned Emmys for comedy writing in 1982 and 1983 for his contributions to the show.

Moranis's more recent work includes 'Streets of Fire' for director Walter Hill, as well as the forthcoming 'The Breakfast Club' and 'The Wild Life.'

About the Filmmakers . . .

Producer/director IVAN REITMAN continues to shape America's perception of contemporary comedy. From the groundbreaking off-Broadway 'National Lampoon Show' to the influential blockbuster 'Animal House,' from the hilarious 'Meatballs' to the international success of 'Stripes,' Reitman's films have become a kind of standard by which movie comedy is measured.

A native Czech whose family fled to Canada when he was four, Reitman accomplished much at an early age. After winning a music prize in a national student competition for the Canadian Bicentennial and producing and directing several shorts in college which were aired on Canadian television, Reitman started New Cinema of Canada, a non-theatrical film distribution company which is still active.

Reitman produced a live television variety show, 'Greed,' and the announcer was a young comedian, Dan Aykroyd. Shortly thereafter, he produced 'Spellbound' for the Toronto stage, which evolved into 'The Magic Show,' a five-year hit on Broadway and the thirteenth longest-running show in Broadway history.

After 'The Magic Show,' Reitman produced the off-Broadway hit, 'The National Lampoon Show,' and its subsequent year-long tour. The success of this show led to the development of 'National Lampoon's Animal House,' which Reitman produced. Released in 1978, this wild comedy became one of the fifteen top-grossing films of all time.

Reitman followed this success with another summer release the next year, 'Meatballs,' starring Bill Murray, which Reitman directed and Harold Ramis co-wrote. In 1981 Reitman struck gold twice, first with the surprise hit of that summer, 'Stripes' (again with Bill Murray and co-starring Harold Ramis, who also co-wrote), followed by the critically acclaimed feature-length animated hit, 'Heavy Metal,' which he produced.

In early 1983, Reitman returned to the Broadway stage, earning a Tony nomination for directing the hit musical magic show, 'Merlin,' which he also produced, starring Doug Henning.

JOHN DE CUIR, production designer for 'Ghostbusters,' is one of the tops in his field, with credits including such memorable films as 'Daddy-Long-Legs,' 'South Pacific,' 'Cleopatra,' 'The Agony and the Ecstasy,' 'On a Clear Day You Can See Forever,' 'The Great White Hope,' 'Hello, Dolly!,' 'Once Is Not Enough,' 'That's Entertainment,' 'The Other Side of Midnight,' and, more recently, 'Raise the Titanic,' 'Dead Men Don't Wear Plaid' and 'Monsignor.' De Cuir has received eleven Academy Award nominations and has won three Oscars for art direction of 'The King and I' (1956), 'Cleopatra' (1963) and 'Hello, Dolly!' (1969).

A graduate of U.S.C. Film School, RICHARD EDLUND has been involved in special visual effects for some of the most successful science fiction motion pictures and television shows in history, including 'The Outer Limits,' 'Twilight Zone' and 'Star Trek' for television, and such hits as 'The China Syndrome,'

'Poltergeist,' 'Star Wars,' 'The Empire Strikes Back,' 'Raiders of the Lost Ark' and 'Return of the Jedi,' the last four of which garnered Academy Awards for Edlund.

Director of photography LASZLO KOVACS has a most impressive list of film credits, including 'Easy Rider,' 'Five Easy Pieces,' 'What's Up Doc?,' 'Paper Moon,' 'New York, New York,' 'Paradise Alley,' 'Butch and Sundance, The Early Days,' 'Heart Beat,' 'Inside Moves,' 'The Legend of the Lone Ranger,' 'Frances' and 'Crackers.'

Costume designer THEONI V. ALDREDGE has created the costumes for films from the visually rich 'The Great Gatsby' (for which she won the Oscar for best costume design in 1974) to 'Harry and Walter Go To New York,' 'The Cheap Detective,' 'Network,' 'The Champ,' 'The Rose' and 'Semi-Tough.' On Broadway, her designs can currently be seen in 'La Cage Aux Folles,' 'Dreamgirls' and '42nd Street.'

SHELDON F. KAHN has edited such films as 'The Electric Horseman,' 'Same Time, Next Year,' 'Bloodbrothers,' 'An Enemy of the People' and 'One Flew Over the Cuckoo's Nest,' for which he was nominated for an Academy Award.

GHOSTBUSTERS

THE CAST

Dr. Peter Venkman	BILL MURRAY
Dr. Raymond Stantz	DAN AYKROYD
Dana Barrett	SIGOURNEY WEAVER
Dr. Egon Spengler	HAROLD RAMIS
Louis Tully	RICK MORANIS
Janine Melnitz	ANNIE POTTS
Walter Peck	WILLIAM ATHERTON
Winston Zeddemore	ERNIE HUDSON
Mayor	DAVID MARGULIES
Male Student	STEVEN TASH
Female Student	JENNIFER RUNYON
Gozer	SLAVITZA JOVAN
Hotel Manager	MICHAEL ENSIGN
Librarian	ALICE DRUMMOND
Dean Yaeger	JORDAN CHARNEY
Violinist	TIMOTHY CARHART
Library Administrator	JOHN ROTHMAN
Archbishop	TOM McDERMOTT
Roger Grimsby	HIMSELF
Larry King	HIMSELF
Joe Franklin	HIMSELF
Casey Kasem	HIMSELF
Fire Commissioner	NORMAN MATLOCK
Police Captain	JOE CIRILLO
Police Sergeant	JOE SCHMIEG
Jail Guard	REGGIE VEL JOHNSON
Real Estate Woman	RHODA GEMIGNANI
Man at Elevator	MURRAY RUBIN

Con Edison Man	LARRY DILG
Coachman	DANNY STONE
Woman at Party	PATTY DWORKIN
Tall Woman at Party	JEAN KASEM
Doorman	LENNY DEL GENIO
Chambermaid	FRANCES E. NEALY
Hot Dog Vendor	SAM MOSES
TV Reporter	CHRISTOPHER WYNKOOP
Businessman in Cab	WINSTON MAY
Mayor's Aide	TOMMY HOLLIS
Louis's Neighbour	EDA REISS MERIN
Policeman at Apartment	RIC MANCINI
Mrs. Van Hoffman	KATHRYN JANSSEN
Reporters	STANLEY GROVER
	CAROL ANN HENRY
	JAMES HARDIE
	FRANTZ TURNER
	NANCY KELLY
Ted Fleming	PAUL TRAFAS
Annette Fleming	CHERYL BIRCHFIELD
Library Ghost	RUTH OLIVER
Dream Ghost	KYM HERRIN
Stunt Coordinator	BILL COUCH

THE CREDITS

Directed by	IVAN REITMAN
Written by	DAN AYKROYD
	HAROLD RAMIS
Produced by	IVAN REITMAN
Director of Photography	LASZLO KOVACS, A.S.C
Production Design by	JOHN DE CUIR
Film Edited by	SHELDON KAHN, A.C.E
	with DAVID BLEWITT, A.C.E
Executive Producer	BERNIE BRILLSTEIN
Associate Producers	JOE MEDJUCK
	MICHAEL C. GROSS
Visual Effects by	RICHARD EDLUND, A.S.C.
Music by	ELMER BERNSTEIN
'Ghostbusters' Written and	
Performed by	RAY PARKER, JR.
Costumes by	THEONI V. ALDREDGE
Casting by	KAREN REA
Production Manager	JOHN G. WILSON
1st Assistant Director	GARY DAIGLER
2nd Assistant Director	KATTERLI FRAUENFELDER
Camera Operator	BOB STEVENS
1st Assistant Cameraman	JOE THIBO
2nd Assistant Cameraman	PAUL MINDRUP
Script Supervisor	TRISH KINNEY
Special Effects Supervisor	CHUCK GASPAR
Special Effects Foreman	JOE DAY
Art Director	JOHN DE CUIR, JR.
Set Designer	GEORGE ECKERT
Set Decorator	MARVIN MARCH

185

Property Master	JACK E. ACKERMAN
Costume Supervisor	BRUCE ERICKSON
Costumers	DAYTON ANDERSON
	PEGGY THORIN
Make-up Artist	LEONARD ENGELMAN
Hair Stylist	DIONE TAYLOR
Gaffer	COLIN CAMPBELL
Best Boy	ROBERT JASON
Key Grip	GENE KEARNEY
Grip Best Boy	BOB MUNOZ
Construction Coordinator	DON NOBLE
Standby Painter	PAUL CAMPANELLA
Transportation Coordinator	JIM FOOTE
Driver Captain	JOHN F. CURTIS
Location Manager	PAUL PAV
Production Coordinator	RITA MILLER-GRANT
Assistant Production Coordinator	SHERRY LYNNE
DGA Trainee	PATRICK McKEE
Production Accountant	KIRK BORCHERDING
Still Photographer	GEMMA LA MANA-WILLS
Publicist	NANCY WILLEN
Secretary to Mr. Reitman	JOYCE Y. IRBY
Secretary to Mr. Gross, Mr. Medjuck	
	KATHI FREEMAN
Optical Effects Administrator	LEONA PHILLIPS
Hardware Consultants	
	STEVEN DANE, JOHN DAVEIKIS
Sound Designers	
	RICHARD BEGGS, TOM McCARTHY, JR.
Assistant Editors	SAUL SALADOW,
	JIM SEIDELMAN, JOE MOSCA
Sound Editing	EFFECTIVE SOUND UNLIMITED
Sound Editors	
	DON S. WALDEN, WILLIAM L. MANGER,
	MIKE REDBOURN, JOSEPH HOLSEN,
	JIM BULLOCK, JOHN COLWELL

Ghostbusters

Production Sound Mixer	GENE CANTAMESSA
Sound Boom	PAUL A. BRUCE
Cableman	JACK WALPA
Re-recording Mixers	LES FRESHOLTZ, C.A.S.

DICK ALEXANDER, C.A.S., VERN POORE, C.A.S

Scoring Mixer	ROBERT FERNANDEZ
Orchestrators	PETER BERNSTEIN, DAVID SPEAR
Supervising Music Editor	

KATHY DURNING, SEGUE MUSIC

NEW YORK CREW

Unit Production Manager	PATRICK McCORMICK
1st Assistant Director	PETER GIULIANO
2nd Assistant Directors	

JOHN PEPPER, BILL EUSTACE

Art Director	JOHN MOORE
Casting by	JOY TODD
Production Coordinator	KATE GUINZBURG
Location Managers	LENNY VULLO, JEFF STOLOW
Wardrobe Supervisors	

LEE AUSTIN, DEBRA LOUIS KATZ

Director of Photography	HERB WAGREITCH
1st Assistant Cameraman	VINCENT GERARDO
2nd Assistant Cameraman	PATRICK CAPONE
Steadicam Operator	TED CHURCHILL
Still Photographer	MICHAEL GINSBURG
Gaffer	BILLY WARD
Key Grip	NORMAN BUCK
Property Master	JOE CARRACCIOLA, JR.
Set Decorator	ROBERT DRUMHELLER
Make-up Artist	MICHAEL THOMAS
Teamster Captain	ROCCO DERASMO
DGA Trainee	CAROL VITKEY
Main Title Animation by	

R/GREENBERG ASSOCS., INC.

Titles by	PACIFIC TITLE

ENTERTAINMENT EFFECTS GROUP,
LOS ANGELES

Visual Effects Art Director	JOHN BRUNO
Visual Effects Editor	CONRAD BUFF
Matte Department Supervisor	NEIL KREPELA
Mechanical Effects Supervisor	THAINE MORRIS
Chief Cameraman	BILL NEIL
Director of Special Projects	GARY PLATEK
Model Shop Supervisor	MARK STETSON
Optical Supervisor	MARK VARGO

Animation Supervisors
GARRY WALLER, TERRY WINDELL

Chief Engineer	GENE WHITEMAN
Chief Matte Artist	MATT YURICICH
Head of Ghost Shop	STUART ZIFF
Godfather	JIM NELSON
Production Supervisor	RICHARD KERRIGAN
Production Coordinator	LAURA BUFF

Camera Operators
JIM AUPPERLE, JOHN LAMBERT

Assistant Cameramen   PETE ROMANO,
JODY WESTHEIMER, CLINT PALMER

Still Photographer   VIRGIL MIRANO

Optical Printer Operators   CHUCK COWLES,
BRUNO GEORGE, BOB WILSON

Optical Line-up   PHIL BARBERIO,
MARY E. WALTER, RONALD B. MOORE

Dimensional Animation Effects   RANDALL W. COOK

Animators   SEAN NEWTON, WILLIAM RECINOS,
BRUCE WOODSIDE, RICHARD COLEMAN

Technical Animators
ANNICK THERREIN, PEGGY REGAN,
SAM RECINOS, PETE LANGTON,
LES BERNSTEIN, WENDIE FISCHER

Additional Animation   AVAILABLE LIGHT LTD.

Assistant Matte Cameraman   ALAN HARDING

Matte Artists
    MICHELLE MOEN. CONSTANTINE GANAKES
Effects Man   ROBERT SPURLOCK
Ghost Shop Advisor   JON BERG
Sculptors   STEVE NEILL, MIKE HOSCH
Onion Head/Librarian Sculptor   STEVE JOHNSON
Staypuft Sculptors   LINDA FROBOS, BILL BRYAN
Chief Moldmaker   GUNNAR FERDINANDSEN
Chief Mechanism Designer   STEVE DUNHAM
Mechanism Designers   DON CARNER,
        JOHN ALBERTI, NICHOLAS ALBERTI,
        DOUG BESWICK, LANCE ANDERSON
Mechanism Builders   JOE FRANKE,
        KEVIN DIXON, TOM CULNAN,
        BILL STURGEON, LARZ ANDERSON
Model Makers   GARY BIEREND, LESLIE EKKER,
        KENT GEBO, PETE GERARD,
        BOB HOFFMAN, PAT McCLUNG,
        DON PENNINGTON, MILIUS ROMYN,
        NICK SELDON, PAUL SKYLAR
Creature Design Consultants   BRENT BOATES,
        TERRY WINDELL, THOM ENRIQUEZ,
        BERNI WRIGHTSON, ROBERT KLINE,
        KURT W. CONNER
Design Engineers   MIKE BOLLES, MARK WEST
Electronics Engineers
        JERRY JEFFRESS, ROBIN LEYDEN
Software Programmer   KRIS BROWN
Production Secretaries   LAUREL WALTER,
        LESLIE FALKINBURG, MARY MASON

MUSIC

'SAVIN' THE DAY'
Written by Bobby Alessi and Dave Immer
Produced by Phil Ramone
Performed by Alessi

'HOT NIGHT'
Written by Diane Warren and The Doctor
Produced by Jack White and Robbie Buchanan
Performed by Laura Branigan

'DISCO INFERNO'
Written by Leroy Green and Ron Kersey
Produced by Ron Kersey
Performed by The Trammps

Laura Branigan and The Trammps
Courtesy of Atlantic Recording Corp.
by arrangement with Warner Special Products

'CLEANIN' UP THE TOWN'
Written by Kevin O'Neal and Brian O'Neal
Produced by Kevin O'Neal, Brian O'Neal and John Hug
Performed by The Bus Boys

'IN THE NAME OF LOVE'
Written by T. Bailey
Produced by Steve Lillywhite
Performed by Thompson Twins

'I CAN WAIT FOREVER'
Written by Graham Russell, David Foster and
Jay Graydon
Produced by David Foster and Jay Graydon
Performed by Air Supply

'MAGIC'
Written by Mick Smiley
Produced by Keith Forsey
Performed by Mick Smiley

Ray Parker, Jr., The Bus Boys, Thompson Twins, and Air Supply appear courtesy of Arista Records. Inc.

Original Soundtrack Album available on
ARISTA RECORDS

The producers wish to thank the New York Office for Motion Pictures and Television Production.
   Thanks also to Suzy Benzinger, Will Fowler, Amy Friedman, Frank Krenz, Hal Landaker, Joanna Lipari, The Los Angeles Public Library, Peggy Semtob, Don Shay and Chris Stoia.

Filmed in Panavision (R)   Metrocolor (R)
FROM COLUMBIA-DELPHI PRODUCTIONS
Copyright © 1984 Columbia Pictures Industries, Inc.
All Rights Reserved
A COLUMBIA PICTURES PRESENTATION
A BLACK RHINO/BERNIE BRILLSTEIN
PRODUCTION
AN IVAN REITMAN FILM

191